ASH

FALLEN

ASH

FALLEN

BLAKE CHANNELS

Blossom Cove Publishing

Ash Fallen. Copyright © 2019 by Blake Channels.

Cover art by Zauberschmeterling and tiky224.

Cover and map design by J&R Brown.

Published by Blossom Cove Publishing™.

To find out more about the author and available books, visit blakechannels.com.

For Kiersten and Bella –

Shine bright and dream big.

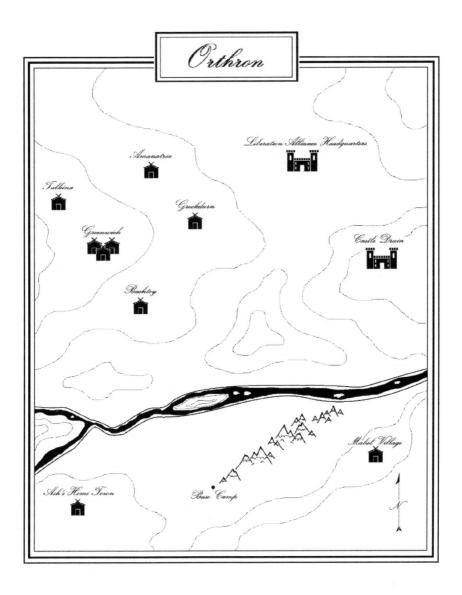

Orthron

CHAPTER ONE

Rosalie parted her lips and tried to mimic her friends and neighbors. Their glassy eyes were focused forward, shoulders slack, as they swayed back and forth like a worn-out porch swing in a gentle, midday breeze. The people of Mabel Village stood in the middle of town square, open-mouthed, but silent; eyes wide open, yet unseeing.

Before chaos erupted, Rosalie had just returned from a morning hunt and was enjoying a late, quiet breakfast on her front porch. She'd always preferred the tranquility of her small village over the buzz and noise of the more populated towns on Orthron. She'd looked up, startled, when she'd heard a whooshing sound and had watched in shock as silver, metal canisters soared through the air and landed on the street in front of her with a resounding clang. A gaseous substance poured from the containers.

Abandoning her blueberry pancakes and piping hot mug of krisha tea, she'd rushed down her porch steps to investigate. Coughing, and vision clouded by the gas, she'd stumbled around in confusion as she'd witnessed the personality changes of her neighbors. While her senses had heightened under the uncertain danger of the vaporous substance, everyone else's seemed to dull. Through the haze, she'd noticed the soldiers swarming the town.

Her heart had skipped a beat as she surveyed her surroundings. The townspeople hadn't appeared worried. In fact, they hadn't shown any emotion. Without speaking, they'd pressed together, eyes fixated ahead as they'd stepped in unison towards town square. Her inquisitiveness getting the better of her, she'd fallen into step with them.

Now she feigned submission as her long, dark auburn hair whipped around her face in the cool morning breeze. Soft tendrils tickled her cheeks and forehead, but she resisted the urge to brush them aside. Just as she resisted the urge to hug her arms to her body to warm herself against the morning chill, or to fiddle with the emerald stone that hung around her neck – something she often did when she felt anxious. Instead, she stood, dark-green eyes unblinking. Heart pounding.

"We need to gather everyone closer," she heard a man's surly voice from somewhere behind her. It was a voice she didn't recognize. Her skin prickled, but despite her curiosity, she resisted the urge to turn her head to investigate.

"Roe," she heard another man whisper. Fear walked down her spine as she fought to ignore the voice. "Roe," the man repeated more forcefully; but this time she recognized who spoke.

"Talon?" she whispered back, still facing forward.

"I'm here." Her loyal, childhood friend appeared at her side, his steady fingers grazing hers. The pair kept their arms at their sides and eyes frontward.

She spoke softly, keeping her voice low. "What's going on with everyone, Talon? I'm scared."

"Shh. Me too," he said, though she'd never known him to show fear and suspected his confession might be exaggerated for her benefit. "I think those canisters launched over the wall weren't just filled with tear gas. I think they held a chemical agent to control us. Everyone is acting like they're sleepwalking."

Rosalie's eyes and nostrils burned from the gas. She was about to ask why the effects of the gas didn't work on the two of them, but noticed the crowd shuffling forward, murmuring as they went. She thought she made out the phrase: *stay the course, be true to the cause.*

"Stay the course, be true to the cause," she muttered in unison as she edged forward, doing her best to blend in with the others.

Talon joined in. "Stay the course, be true to the cause." He kept his tone flat.

The crowd pressed together under the ancient oak tree outside the red-bricked building of Mabel City Hall. A thick, morning fog cloaked the square and the air was dense with the smell of sweat and rotting grass clippings. Rosalie felt cramped and fought against the urge to panic as the throng squeezed closer together. The murmuring ceased, and the group once again swayed back and forth, back and forth.

Two men approached the swaying villagers. Both appeared threatening – armed and intense. Their tall stature and broad-shouldered, brawny build suggested their presence should not be taken lightly. Behind them, they were flanked by a small army. The soldiers didn't carry shields or wear fancy breast plates. Instead, they were dressed in protective leather skins and armed mostly with spears or bows. Some held daggers and swords. Few held guns. Under normal circumstances, Rosalie thought her village might have stood a chance against these men and their crude weapons. But under the powers of whatever drug controlled the town-folk, there was little hope.

The man with the dark-red hair moved through the crowd, analyzing each villager. He spoke softly as he stared into the vacant eyes of each person. Rosalie's spine tingled. Would he realize the gas hadn't worked on her? Beside her, Talon gave her hand a reassuring squeeze, then dropped his hand back to his side.

After what seemed like an hour, but was likely less than ten minutes, the man made his way over to Rosalie and Talon. He towered above them, and beads of perspiration formed on Rosalie's forehead. Beside her, she could hear Talon's breathing patterns change. His breath became shallow, labored.

After looking each of them in the eye, a look of surprise crossed the man's face. And then he smiled a peculiar smile. He turned to his right and motioned to one of his men. "These two," he said, pointing at Talon and Rosalie. "Bring them up the steps."

Talon squeezed Rosalie's hand once more as the pair was led up the concrete steps of City Hall. His hand was clammy in hers. "I'll be fine. We'll be fine," she heard herself say. But her words lacked confidence.

CHAPTER TWO

Rosalie studied the two, fierce men who stood before her atop the steps of City Hall. The man on the left, whom she'd heard called Stryker, appeared to be the leader. He peered back at her through his dark, wicked eyes. His hair was blonde, almost white. A deep scar ran down his right cheek and stopped above his jawline. He wore his hair long on one side, partially covering the scar.

On Stryker's right was the man who'd picked her and Talon out of the crowd. He was a tall, muscular man with dark-red, tousled hair cropped below his ears. Rosalie gathered he was second-in-command. He was handsome, in a brusque, mysterious sort of way. He had a confident air about him. He wore khaki-colored shorts, and when he turned to address the men, Rosalie noticed the tattoo of a dagger covering his left calf muscle. She was always drawn to the dangerous types, and she bit her lip, intrigued despite the magnitude of her situation.

The two leaders exchanged a meaningful look before the man with the tattoo approached Rosalie. She tried not to flinch as he studied her.

When he held her gaze with his icy blue eyes, he appeared to see right through her.

"I'm Ash," he said briskly.

She stared coolly back at him, unblinking.

"What's your name?" he ordered. His tone was commanding and unfriendly.

"Rosalie," she said, squaring her shoulders.

"Rosalie, you will come with us. I can either bind you and see you carried off, or you can come willingly."

"I'll come willingly." She tried to sound brave, but the quiver in her voice was undeniable. She bit the inside of her lip to keep it from trembling.

"Look through the homes. Take what you can find that will be of use to us," the man named Stryker barked to a group of men standing a few steps below. The men dispersed to carry out the order.

"Please, please don't leave them defenseless," Rosalie begged, eyes glistening with tears.

"We need the weapons," Ash explained. When she started to protest, and his eyes met hers, he found himself softening. "We'll leave enough behind for them to protect themselves." Then he motioned to one of his men. The man ran up the steps, two at a time. When he reached the top, Ash murmured something in his ear. A questioning look crossed the man's face, but he masked it quickly, nodded in response, then turned and jogged in the direction of the others.

"Thank you," Rosalie whispered. Ash grunted, claiming indifference with a shrug of his shoulders, then walked down the steps. The villagers had grown quiet and were standing ramrod straight, still facing City Hall. When he reached the bottom step, he spoke in hushed tones. Rosalie couldn't hear his words, but she felt oddly comforted by the soothing sound of his voice.

"Let's move out," Stryker ordered once the men returned with their loot.

Ash grabbed the canteen one of the men handed him and offered it to Rosalie. When she refused it, he thrust it into her hands. "You'd only be hurting yourself."

She snatched it from him, slipped the strap over her shoulder, then fell into step behind him. Talon walked beside her, keeping quiet. His wrists were bound – but thankfully his feet were not, and he wasn't gagged. Rosalie knew he couldn't bear the shame of being gagged or forced to hobble. She walked in silence, all the while sending up silent prayers to Evgund, god of protection and morality.

When they reached base camp, it was growing dusk. Unlike Mabel Village, base camp was a poorer township, void of modern amenities. Instead of stick-built or brick homes with glowing porchlights, there was a circle of modest grass huts with flaming torches to mark the entrances.

Stryker and Ash disappeared into separate huts and Rosalie and Talon were led to a campfire to warm themselves. Both sat warily on an overturned log being used as a makeshift bench. Exhausted from the journey and unsure of their emotional state, neither spoke. Rosalie's feet ached from the long walk. The terrain had been rough, and the leather, worn-out ankle boots she'd worn were hardly appropriate footwear. Perhaps if she'd known she'd be walking all day, she would have chosen different shoes. Then again, she thought, if she'd known what was going to happen when she awoke that morning, she probably would have stayed in bed. Or hid beneath it.

She and Talon were given a meager bowl of stringy stew. They shared the remaining water in the canteen. Rosalie rarely ate anything she didn't hunt or grow herself, but given her mounting hunger pains, she made a singular exception. The stew was flavorless, and smelled unpleasant, but the pair scarfed it down wholeheartedly. Neither knew when their next meal was coming – or *if* it was coming.

After dinner, the two friends were separated. Talon was placed in a guarded hut with a handful of prisoners, but Rosalie was led to a smaller hut. When she entered the humble dwelling with the straw roof and dirt floors, she saw Ash standing in the corner. He was leaning over a rickety table and studying a map by candlelight. Whenever he moved, his muscles rippled from beneath his tight shirt.

Forgetting her tired feet, Rosalie shifted tactics. As she approached him, she pushed out her chest, taking a flirty, unfiltered approach.

"Where is your leader?" she crooned.

"My leader?" he asked, giving her a blank stare.

"Yes, the man they call Stryker."

A devious smile played across his lips. "My *leader*," he said, "is elsewhere. You're here to tell me what you know about Castle Druin."

"What would you like to know?" She let her hand rest on his chest, then playfully trailed her fingers down his abdomen.

He caught her hand before she could explore further, pressing his thumb hard against the veins in her wrist.

"Careful now," he warned, giving her wrist a squeeze and finding pleasure in the escalated rhythm of her pulse. "Stryker will be in no mood for your games." His grip was strong, and she involuntarily shuddered at his touch.

"And what are you in the mood for?" she taunted, testing him. Her voice was sultry – low, yet wildly feminine.

"I'm in the mood for you to tell me about Druin," he said, releasing his hold on her wrist and taking a step back from her. His pointed stare penetrated her thin shield of false confidence.

She shrugged her shoulders, trying to appear unphased. "I don't know much about it."

"You lie," Ash said, matter-of-fact. "Your village has been at odds with the Druin ruler for decades. You appear to be one of the warriors," he said as he skimmed his fingers over one of the leather strips of her shockingly short skirt, "so I'd say that makes you an expert."

Rosalie rewarded him with a playful smile, but her heart pounded in her chest. Though she'd heard unspeakable stories about Lord Zebadiah, ruler of the Druins, and his harsh treatment of his people, she'd never set foot on Druin soil. Her captor must have misread her attire as that of a warrior. She was a huntress, which meant she could be rather resourceful, but she was no warrior. The overall look was similar she supposed – sleeveless, button-up shirt knotted above the waistline and leather, gladiator-style skirt. But the bold stitching and intricate beadwork of a female warrior's skirts easily set them apart from the simplicity of those worn by a huntress.

"And what do I get out of this if I tell you?" she said, feeling less smug.

"You get to live." He kept his tone low and flat. "I'll give you some time to consider it." He returned his attention to the map, dismissing her with a flick of his wrist.

Rosalie left the hut, shell-shocked. She wasn't accustomed to being so easily discarded. Fear and uncertainty settled in the pit of her stomach.

A lanky, sandy-haired man stood outside the hut, waiting to escort her to her sleeping quarters. He smiled at her, but it wasn't a friendly smile; more like a smirk.

"You can't be serious," she said, once she saw where her captors intended to keep her. Her new home was to be a cramped, make-shift cell shared with four male detainees. She tried to keep the panic out of her voice when she heard the vulgar catcalls from the prisoners.

"Take me back to Ash," she spoke with authority to the man at her side. She placed her hands on her hips to keep them from shaking.

"Ash doesn't have any use for you," he said, growing impatient.

"I have information he'll find useful."

The man hesitated and doubt clouded his features.

"I'm a Mender," she blurted out in desperation.

This did pique the man's interest. "A Mender, you say?" His tone was a blend of fascination and skepticism.

"Yes," she said, with mounting confidence. "Your men look like they're planning to go to battle. My mending powers can be of service."

After pausing to consider, the man grabbed her by the arm. "Very well then, I'll take you back to Ash. But I'll warn you, he's not to be trifled with. If you are exaggerating your powers, you will regret it."

When Rosalie reentered Ash's hut, she was more humbled, but fire still burned in her eyes. Ash continued to pour over the brittle map and pretended not to notice her presence, but he smiled to himself. With her auburn hair that stopped above her waist, athletic figure, and scantily clad attire, the woman was stunning. Intriguing. Trouble. He figured she probably broke every heart and rule she ever came across.

"Back so soon?" he tormented, still feigning disinterest.

"She's a *disparate*," the man at Rosalie's side revealed.

Ash's eyes flitted to Rosalie's, then he flashed the man a warning look. "I don't care for that term," he said flatly.

The man flushed red and his shoulders slumped. Rosalie would have smirked with satisfaction if she wasn't so uncertain of her own fate. "She's a *variant*," he corrected himself. "Claims to be a Mender."

"I see," Ash said, addressing him but looking over at Rosalie. The anger in his eyes had cooled. "Leave us, then."

When they were alone, he came around the table and stood before her. She couldn't help but feel small as he towered above her. "A Mender, huh?"

He scrutinized her. After a half-century of purity crusades, tens of thousands of *variants* (the lawful term given to people with powers) were hunted down and killed. They were called disparate, deviants, mutants – "the un-pure." The women suffered most. Accused of calling on evil spirits to wield their powers, they were met with unspeakable deaths.

The crusades ended decades prior, but the *variants* who remained often kept their powers hidden, out of survival for the most part.

Although they were awarded equal rights and laws were enacted to keep them safe, they still battled discrimination and people's fear of the unknown. Ash was surprised she gave up the information so willingly. The thought of spending the evening in cramped quarters with ill-mannered men must have frightened her. He'd speculated that it might do the trick.

"A Mender, and a Soother, actually," she said, holding her head high.

He crossed his arms in front of his chest. "Prove it."

"How would you like me to prove it?" she demanded, raising an eyebrow. She placed her hands on her hips, then quickly returned them to her sides when she realized the gesture drew her captor's attention to her bare midsection.

His gaze lingered on her slender, toned waist, then, as if finally realizing he was gawking, he returned his focus to her eyes. "I was thrown from a horse a few days ago. I tweaked my back. I want you to make it feel better."

"Speaking of horses," she said, side-stepping his concentrated stare, "I couldn't help but notice the rather impressive pack of horses at your disposal. Was there a reason we had to walk today?"

"I like to keep the horses rested when we have less than a day's journey. Now can you help me out or not?" He sensed she might be stalling.

"Fine. I'll need you to close your eyes."

"And let you sucker punch me and run away? There's no chance of that," he chuckled.

Rosalie's shoulders slumped as her chances of escape dulled. "Okay, well I'll need to close my eyes, so I'll need your word you won't try anything."

His blue eyes pierced hers. "You have my word."

She could tell he was being truthful. The intensity of his stare made her shudder, but it wasn't in fear. She held his gaze, refusing to back down. "Take off your shirt and turn around."

Ash obeyed, slipping off his shirt and offering her his bare back. After taking in his tan, muscular form, she closed her eyes in concentration. She placed both hands flat against his back and moved them slowly until she felt the site of the injury. She could always find the spot. Injuries had their own energy. Closing her eyes, she whispered a soft chant.

As she recited the words, Ash felt a chill, then a rush of warmth down his spine – then, relief. When the pain lifted, he turned to her and smiled in amazement. The smile was genuine, revealing a small dimple below his left cheek. "You fixed it." He twisted from side to side without discomfort, then turned again to face her.

"Careful now," she warned. "I'm not a Healer. I soothed the pain and facilitated the mending process, that's all. You should be right as rain in a week or two, but the pain may return before then. The soothing charm only lasts for so long."

"You're going to stay here until I'm better then."

She took a step backwards, her eyes narrowing in suspicion. She was partially relieved she wouldn't spend her nights in a prison cell. But she also didn't need this brute of a man assuming he could do with her as he pleased.

"I will have a separate cot brought in," he clarified.

A blush crept across her cheeks. "I agree then."

"Sweetheart, I wasn't giving you a choice."

Once a cot and blankets were brought in, Rosalie busied herself preparing for bed. She brushed her teeth with her index finger and untangled her hair with her fingertips. When she slipped under the covers, fully clothed except her shoes, Ash approached her – rope in hand.

"And just what do you intend to do with that?"

"I'm afraid it's necessary." His mouth curved downward in an apologetic frown.

"You can't be serious."

"I need to make sure you don't run off. Or try and do me in while I sleep. It's either this," he said, skimming his fingers over the rope, "or I can put you in that fancy cell you saw earlier. Your choice."

Rosalie's bravery faltered, and her bottom lip trembled. She knew nothing about this man or his intentions. Once he bound her, there would be nothing to stop him from doing with her as he pleased. Terror gripped her body and clawed at her throat. As he came closer, she held her breath, her body paralyzed by fear. She stared into the icy abyss of her captor's eyes, at a loss for words. "Please," she managed.

Ash studied the way her eyes shone when she was frightened. The tears she held back glistened against the green of each iris. It angered him that he noticed such an insignificant detail. "If you're worried I'll try something, you've got it all wrong," he said gruffly. "I'm not that desperate and frankly, you're not my type."

If he was trying to provoke her to lessen her fear, it worked. Anger flashed in her eyes and she thrust her wrists upwards and towards him.

His gruffness dissipated and he softened his tone. "I'll keep one hand free, okay?"

She shrugged as if it made no difference to her, but there was no mistaking her visible relief.

When he leaned in to bind her, he caught the intoxicating smell of sandalwood and jasmine – a stimulating blend of spicy and sweet. He closed his eyes and struggled to maintain his composure. With quick movements, he wrapped the rope around her left wrist, then tied the end of the rope to a hook on the wall. He fashioned a brass bell to the rope. When Rosalie struggled against it, the bell clanged.

"With one hand untied, I'm sure you'll be able to free yourself, but this bell will be my alarm if you try."

When he tapped the bell with his index finger, she shot him a withering look. She wanted nothing more than to punch him; to see his look of surprise when her fist connected with his beautiful jawline. With her free hand, she punched the pillow instead.

CHAPTER THREE

Ash ducked out of the hut to cool down. His body begged for sleep, but he needed a walk and the crisp night air to clear his head. He'd meant it when he said Rosalie wasn't his type, though he hadn't intended it as an insult. Typically, he was drawn to carefree women he couldn't see a future with – women who, like him, weren't looking for long-term. Rosalie didn't fit the part. Despite her cool exterior, flirty behavior, and flagrant disregard for modesty, he suspected she was a one-man woman. The marrying type. The worst kind. He'd need to keep his distance; for both their sakes.

He'd seen more attractive women before, although he couldn't recall when. He thought back to the moment his eyes first met hers. The brilliant green of her almond-shaped eyes had softened his defenses. Her delicate face was a staggering contrast to her brazen temperament. She was already causing him to do things he wouldn't ordinarily do – leaving weapons behind at her village, having her stay in his room instead of putting her with the other prisoners. Okay, perhaps he couldn't blame her for that last part. It wasn't her fault his flesh was weaker than he had realized.

The three moons of Orthron lit up the night sky above him. His breath froze in mid-air as he exhaled, but he felt blanketed by an unexplainable heat. It had taken all his willpower not to kiss her when he had her alone. He imagined how she would taste – a maddening blend of sweet, yet salty after the day's journey. Her intoxicating scent of sandalwood and jasmine still lingered, leaving him spiraling.

He headed towards Stryker's hut, but changed his mind before he reached it. He knew his friend didn't approve of him taking Rosalie with them. If it were up to Stryker, they would have dumped her at the next village, despite the plan at hand. The female presence was a dangerous distraction in a camp full of men. He headed for Marx's hut instead – the one person who agreed with Rosalie's presence in the camp; though Marx's reasons for keeping her around were less complicated than Ash's.

Despite his attempts to avoid Stryker, the two men met up outside Marx's hut.

"Don't worry about it. She's my problem," Ash said before Stryker could start in on him.

"That's where you're wrong. She's all of our problem."

Ash locked eyes with him and furrowed his brow in concentration.

"Don't even try it," Stryker said, raising an eyebrow.

"Try what?" Ash asked innocently, but a smile tugged at the corners of his mouth.

"You know what you were doing."

"I'm sure I don't know what you mean."

Stryker shook his head in disapproval, but his face split into a wide grin. "Save that wooing trick for the ladies my friend."

Marx opened the door without prompting and invited the two men in. "I saw her brought in," he said once they were behind closed doors. "Pretty." He shot Ash a pointed look.

"Hadn't noticed," Ash countered, but his cheeks warmed, and he flashed a guilty grin.

Marx huffed in reply. He tossed each of his guests a warm beer and popped the top off a third one for himself. "I wouldn't get too close," he cautioned Ash. "You know the reason she's here."

Ash was about to ask why Stryker wasn't getting the same lecture, but instead he nodded and sat on the edge of the bed. His expression was grim, and he took a long swig of the beer. His face contorted when the warm, bitter liquid touched his tongue.

"Nothing is certain," Marx said after several moments of silence passed. Again, his gaze settled on Ash.

Ash grunted in agreement, uncertain if the words were meant to be taken as a warning or encouragement. He hoped for the latter. He drained the remainder of his beer in misery, pretending it was his drink's lack of refrigeration that was responsible for his dark mood.

As he made his way back to the hut, Ash was bleary-eyed, tipsy, and looking for a fight. His foggy discontent melted away, replaced by captivating clarity, when he saw Rosalie lying there. She was fast asleep; her reddish-brown hair splayed across the pillow. She was curled up in a fetal position, and despite her bound wrist, she looked at peace. He studied her cheekbones and pretty mouth. He imagined her lips would be soft; agonized over how she would taste. A sweet nectar of wine and honey. But it wasn't only her beauty that fascinated him. He'd been impressed by the way, despite her fears, she'd stood up for her village – begging him not to leave her people defenseless. It took courage. Courage and compassion.

He bent down and straightened her blanket, covering where her thigh was left partially exposed between the strips of her leather skirt. Unable to stop himself, he lifted a tendril of her hair off her cheek and tucked it behind her ear. He let his fingertips rest against the softness of her skin. When Rosalie sighed in her sleep, and her plump lips parted, Ash sighed too. His father once told him beauty was more dangerous than the blade. He'd disagreed up to this point. Thoughts in turmoil, he crept to his own cot. He had a feeling he was in for a long night.

CHAPTER FOUR

Rosalie's dreams were vivid. She dreamt of fleeing the vast walls of Mabel Village as it went up in smoke. A chorus of voices shouted in anguish as she made her escape, leaving the frightened throng behind to fend for themselves amongst the flames and smoke plumes. She knew she should feel guilty for abandoning her people, but she felt as if she was running towards something as opposed to running away. She edged forward with purpose. And through the smoky haze she saw the one she ran to. She saw Ash.

When she awoke, she bolted upright in bed, disoriented. Her hand flew to her necklace, her fingertips caressing the smooth stone as she glanced around the unfamiliar room to try and collect her bearings. Her neck and body felt tight. She'd slept curled into a ball, a habit whenever she felt troubled or insecure. It was when she began to massage the kink in her neck that she noticed both her hands were free. The rope that had bound her lay limp on the floor; the unwelcome bell lay beside it.

She smiled to herself, realizing Ash must have untied her while she slept. It pleased her more than it should have. She glanced over at his cot and was disappointed to find it empty. It was scarcely dawn.

Rosalie scolded herself. This may be her chance to escape yet instead she lay moping about a man she didn't know and should, by all logic, fear. Scrambling out of bed, she tugged on her shoes, then opened the door, ready to bolt.

"Do you need something?" a man asked. He stood beside the door, leaning casually against the wall of the hut and picking his teeth with a slender, plastic object.

"Got anything to eat around here?" She knew the man recognized the wild look in her eyes and realized she'd planned to make a break for it.

Sparing her pride and doing his best to hide his amusement, the man nodded towards the campfire. "There's some leftovers if you hurry."

She studied him. Was she allowed to wander the camp as she pleased? How many eyes were on her? She couldn't be sure.

"It's not going to grow legs and walk over to you, if that's what you're waiting for," he smirked.

Ignoring his comment, she walked towards the inviting fire. The warmth of the flames beckoned her closer. A handful of men stood beside it, warming their hands and jawing. But most men were busy breaking camp and packing up the horses.

She approached an elderly man sitting close to the fire, poking at the smoldering logs with a long, wooden stick. "Where is everybody going?"

"You mean, where are *we* going? We're headed to the next base camp, as planned."

"You mean this isn't where you live?" Her tone was a blend of confusion and relief.

"This hovel? No. This was an abandoned township we made into a base camp while we scouted out the nearby villages."

"So you could plunder them." Rosalie spoke sharp, not bothering to keep the disdain out of her tone. It sickened her to think of what may have happened to her village after she'd been taken away. Her mind flashed back to her dream. *Had her village been burned?*

The man looked up at her. He rubbed his chin in thought as if he contemplated arguing with her. Seeming to change his mind, he went back to poking at the fire with his stick.

Realizing she wouldn't get any more out of him, Rosalie plucked a plate from a stack on a tree stump and proceeded to dish up a porridge-like substance from the black kettle suspended above the fire. She glanced around for utensils. Finding none, she sat on a fallen log and began to eat, shoveling the food into her mouth with her fingertips.

"Very ladylike," a man's voice declared from behind her. She jumped and whipped her head around. Ash towered above her, eyes dancing with humor. "I didn't mean to frighten you," he said, stifling a grin.

"You didn't frighten me." She returned her attention to her plate, pretending his presence didn't affect her, but her shaky fingers gave her away as she picked through her food.

He sat beside her, not waiting for an invitation. "How did you sleep?"

"Fine." She didn't return his gaze and silence passed between them. "Thank you for untying me," she mumbled after a long pause.

He shrugged. "We're headed out in a bit. You might want to dress warmer. I put some clothing on the cot that is a bit more … practical."

"More modest?" she said, glancing over at him and raising an eyebrow.

"More comfortable."

"You mean more comfortable for *you*." She knew she shouldn't toy with him, but presently it was the only defensive move she had.

It was obvious her comment unnerved him. He cleared his throat but didn't answer. Instead, he stood to his feet, mumbled something about checking on the horses, and walked away. There was no arguing with her.

She smirked with satisfaction. She'd pegged him perfectly.

When she returned to the hut, she found a change of clothing stacked neatly on the cot. She held up a man's flannel shirt. It was a pale blue; threadbare and faded, but it felt soft and warm against her skin. She held it to her face, inhaling the woodsy, soapy combination and enjoying the tickle of the fabric on her cheek. "More comfortable," she said aloud, smiling to herself.

She glanced around the hut, then removed the knife she kept sheathed beneath the leather folds of her skirt. She stripped off her shirt and skirt and tossed them on the bed beside the knife. She discarded her panties on the floor and smirked at Ash's oversight at not finding her a replacement pair. Then again, she realized, it might not have been an oversight at all.

She stood beside the cot in her bare legs and the button-up flannel shirt as she held up the pants to inspect them. She was pleased to find they were tailored for a woman, but for someone a size or two larger than herself. She pulled them on, then crouched on the dirt floor of the hut to find the rope. Retrieving it, she used her knife to cut off a section of rope, then buried the knife below her discarded clothing.

Rosalie threaded the rope through the beltloops of her pants and tied it in a knot in front. She was swimming in the bulky shirt, but she was grateful for its size. It meant she could hide her weapon. She fastened the sheathed knife to her make-shift rope belt and pulled her shirt over it. Satisfied the knife was properly concealed, she rolled up her shirtsleeves, then sat on the edge of the cot and slipped on her socks and shoes.

"You ready to go?" Ash poked his head into the hut, startling her for the second time that morning. "You're a bit jumpy today," he chuckled.

She stood to her feet, placed her hands on her hips, and glared in his direction but didn't say anything.

He cleared his throat. "We're headed towards Greenwich. I think you'll find our next camp more suitable to your taste." His gaze traveled up and down as he stared in her direction.

She tugged at the hem of her shirt, wondering if he could make out the outline of the knife beneath the flannel fabric. Shifting uncomfortably, she wrestled with the question she longed to ask him. She thought about her dream; about the way the villagers cried out in anguish amongst the smokestacks.

"What became of my village?" she finally blurted out.

A surprised expression flickered across his handsome face. "What do you mean?"

"I mean…" she paused, dreading the answer. "I mean," she spoke more softly, choking on the words, "did you kill them?" Her heart ached as she thought of her neighbors. Mr. Kym with his precious flowerpots he watered faithfully each morning. Vejkie, the little boy across the street who waved at her every day and swore he was going to marry her when he was old enough. Thank the gods her parents and younger brother moved away years ago, enticed to start fresh in Torryn Place with its promises of safety and prosperity.

Ash stepped towards her. It surprised her when he took both of her hands in his. "We didn't kill anyone," he assured her. "The gas we use wears off in a couple hours' time. The people of your village probably came out of it confused and a bit lethargic, but no harm came to them." His eyes met hers. "We left them weapons as you asked, but I don't anticipate they'll need them."

Overwhelmed with relief and gratitude, she fought back the urge to hug her captor. She pulled her hands out of his grasp and shoved them into her pants pockets instead. "I still don't understand what you came for."

A devious smile played across his lips as he considered her question. "Darling, you might say we came for you." Then he turned on his heel and exited the hut. Rosalie sank onto the cot, mystified.

CHAPTER FIVE

During the lengthy journey to Greenwich, Rosalie rode on horseback, seated double behind Ash. She felt guilty each time she glanced back at the wagon that held the other prisoners, including Talon. She'd attempted to see him before they headed out, but the camp had been too chaotic, and Ash had her on a short leash. He probably feared she'd try to escape. He figured correctly.

Her arms were around Ash's waist to keep from toppling off the horse, but she tried to keep her grip loose. She didn't approve of the way her body responded to his warmth or his invigorating scent. She tried not to notice the delectable way his mop of hair curled atop his head. She'd never been partial to redheaded men. But something about Ash made her turn to mush. His no-nonsense, commanding presence turned her on and infuriated her all at once. She knew she needed to get a grip.

She peered over his shoulder and tried to concentrate on her surroundings instead. Everything they passed was picturesque – like something out of a painting. The cloudless sky was a brilliant blue.

Farmlands stretched for miles and glorious, snow-capped mountains stood boldly in the distance. But neither the beauty of the rolling green hills, nor the allure of the freshly cut wheat fields could hold her interest like he could. She sighed heavily to herself.

"Something wrong?"

She hadn't realized her sigh had been audible. Embarrassed, she said, "Just bored."

"We're riding this fine animal through the most beautiful countryside; we couldn't have ordered up better weather, and you're bored?" He shook his head and chuckled softly.

"Maybe it's the company," she snapped, regretting her harsh words the moment she uttered them.

Ash's jaw tightened and the pair rode on in silence.

They spent the first night in canvas tents. Rosalie was given her own tent, although it was surrounded by several others. Ordinarily she preferred to be alone; savored her alone time, even. But that night she spent the lonely hours huddled beneath the blankets, clasping the brilliant stone around her neck as she prayed for warmth and for the gods to help her through whatever her captors had in store for her.

With the higher elevation, though the days were warm enough, the temperatures plummeted in the evenings. Outside, the wind howled and whipped at the tents. The torches surrounding the campsite had all gone out, plunging her world into darkness. She squeezed her eyes shut and concentrated on happier times.

Rosalie grasped for memories that made her feel safe. Her childhood was full of such memories, but they also made her miss her parents and her brother, so she pushed those aside. She thought of the sundrenched days she'd spent with Talon, skipping rocks on the riverbank, spear fishing; making out on some occasions – although, at least for her, it was more out of curiosity than genuine desire. Her feelings for him had always been platonic and she assumed Talon felt the same. She thought of being home, curled up with a book in front of the warm fireplace. But invading her every thought and dream, she thought of Ash.

When dawn broke, Rosalie stumbled out of the tent, looking bleary-eyed and fatigued. As Ash watched her, he noted the dark circles under her eyes and was pleased to see she hadn't slept well. He'd given her enough blankets to keep her protected, but not fully comfortable. He was still smarting from her comment about being bored with his company and wanted her to realize she needed him more than she cared to admit.

He hadn't slept well either, truth be told. He'd spent his night imagining how it would feel to cradle her warm body against his; to caress her soft curves and watch the seductive rise and fall of her chest as she slept peacefully by his side. No matter how hard he tried to keep her out of his head, she got through. He could have sworn he caught the lingering scent of jasmine as he finally drifted off to sleep.

The morning wind slapped at Rosalie's face and sent goosebumps down her arms. She made a beeline toward the inviting campfire, all the while scanning for a glimpse of Talon and the other prisoners. Disappointed at not seeing them, but feeling famished, she took a seat by the warm fire and scarfed down a bowl of mush. She missed homemade blueberry pancakes. She washed down the bland breakfast with lukewarm water, all the while pretending it was a mug of steaming krisha tea.

Her fingers felt numb as she helped break camp, taking special care disassembling and packing her own tent. She still didn't see Talon. She supposed he slept in one of the wagons with the other prisoners and felt another pang of guilt. Then again, she reasoned, he had probably kept warm.

When it was time to go, she didn't refuse Ash's offer to help her up on the horse. She wrapped her hands tightly around his waist and pressed her cheek to his back. She welcomed his heat; imagined how it would have felt to spend the night in his arms. While she concentrated on staying awake, she allowed her thoughts to run wild.

Ash couldn't help himself; he was pleased how it felt to have this auburn-haired vixen pressed up so close to him. He smiled to himself. He took one hand off the reins and patted her delicate hands. When he realized how cold they felt, he gave her right hand a squeeze, then, without thinking, pressed it to his lips. This time when Rosalie sighed, it was a deep, satisfied sigh, and his insides churned with desire.

When the party arrived late-morning at the new base camp in Greenwich, Rosalie couldn't contain her enthusiasm. The site wasn't a town, but rather a deserted, one-story hostel on the outskirts of a forest, just off an abandoned roadway. The peeling green paint and sagging roof suggested the boarding house had been empty for some time.

"I don't suppose there's running water?" she asked Ash, hopeful at the prospect of a shower.

"There is, actually. We have scouts who go ahead and get the camps ready. They make sure they're safe and functional. Some sites are better than others."

Her pretty mouth turned downward into a frown. "You'll plan the raid of more villages from this spot." Her tone was more melancholy than accusatory.

He fell silent. He hated to see her down. Hated even more that she had him all wrong. But now wasn't the time to explain. Ignoring her comment, he dismounted, then held up his arms to help her down from the horse. Refusing his assistance, she made a graceful dismount then headed in the direction of the hostel. She realized her mistake immediately. All the doors faced outwards and she had no idea which room was to be hers. Or whom she would share it with.

She slowed her pace to wait for Ash. He pulled two sugar cubes from his pocket and fed them to his horse – speaking soothingly as he stroked the animal's mane. After handing over the reins to one of the soldiers, he strolled up behind Rosalie and took her by the elbow, leaning in close. "We're in room 4," he spoke into her ear. "I'll join you in a bit."

He jogged off in the direction of the front office, leaving Rosalie wanting to kick herself. His words had sent a chill down her spine – and it wasn't out of fear.

The room was cramped, but clean. Rosalie concluded the scouts must have washed the bedding and tidied up. Although the air was stale, a hint of a lemon-based cleaning solution still lingered. The teal, threadbare carpeting looked vacuumed – though hastily done. She felt a pang of homesickness as she considered how her mother would have disapproved of the wavy vacuum lines.

She did notice there was only one bed and merely a full-sized one at that. She swallowed her panic and redirected her attention to the remainder of the room. A pocket door led to a modest bathroom complete with a shower, toilet, and vanity. She hurried to the sink and turned on the faucet. The pipes creaked and moaned, but before long, clear water poured out. The water was icy cold, but she washed her hands, retrieving soap from the cabinet under the sink. She found bottles of shampoo, conditioner, and tiny packages of toothpaste, toothbrushes, and razors. She wanted to shout her excitement from the sagging rooftops.

She turned on the shower instead. While she was delighted the scouts managed to get the water running, it wasn't hot. She shivered when the cold water pelted her skin, but she leaned her head back and allowed the water to pour over her. She lathered herself in soap and was pleased to discover the razor she'd found wasn't rusted or dulled. She took her time freshening up, temporarily forgetting her plight.

When she stepped out of the shower, she realized her error. In her excitement to get clean, she hadn't checked to see if there were towels. She searched the cabinets. None. Shivering, she knew she'd need to improvise. She was scurrying around the room, naked, when Ash walked in.

At seeing her naked for the first time, he appeared startled and flustered. He diverted his eyes. "I'm sorry," he murmured. Before she could reply, he stepped out of the room and shut the door behind him.

Rosalie was never one to be concerned about showing too much skin. She was comfortable with her body. She laughed to herself at Ash's obvious discomfort. His reaction also gave her relief. It meant she wasn't in danger of him trying anything on her. It was obvious he wasn't that kind of man. So, what sort of man was he? What sort of man went from village to village, not killing anyone, but robbing supplies, kidnapping only a few, and then moving on? Everything about him puzzled her.

After she'd dried herself with the bedsheet, she contemplated putting on the clothes Ash had given her, but reverted to her own clothes instead. She knew the short skirt and shirt knotted above her midsection kept Ash off balance. It was the only power she had over him at present and she was determined to take advantage of it.

She slathered creamy lotion over her smooth, freshly shaved legs. Unable to find a brush, she smoothed out her tangled, wet hair with her fingers instead. She did manage to find a hair tie. She swept her hair into a high ponytail, relieved to have it out of her face.

Once she felt presentable, she wondered if she should attempt to find Talon. A glance out the window revealed a man guarding her doorway. She started to turn away in disappointment when she heard a scuffle outside. She recognized Talon's voice. He was yelling in anger and pain. She flung open the door. Talon and another man were rolling around in the dirt, swinging punches and cursing. She ran in their direction, ready to join in the fight to help her friend.

She was ready to launch herself at the stranger when Ash grabbed her from behind, lifting her off the ground. "Don't," he said.

She kicked her legs in the air, failing to make contact with anything. "Let me go," she screamed.

"He's fine," Ash told her. "Let them work it out."

When he set her down, Rosalie turned to him, glowering. The men continued to scuffle. "You have to put a stop to this," she begged.

"Why?" he grinned. "They're just letting off a little steam."

She shoved him, then turned to help her friend, but quickly learned the aid was unnecessary. Talon stood to his feet, brushing himself off. The man he had fought lay on the ground, bleeding from his mouth and nose. Talon stretched out his hand and helped him to his feet.

When the man raised his fists to fight again, Ash stepped in. "I think we're done here," he spoke sharply. The man lowered his head and shuffled away.

Rosalie looked from Talon to her captor.

"Roe," Talon said in surprise, still panting from the exhilaration of the scuffle. He glared at Ash and his hands balled into fists at his sides.

"I'll give you two a moment," Ash said. He didn't mask his irritation as he turned to walk away.

Once he was gone, Talon pulled Rosalie close, wrapping her in a fierce hug. "I've been so worried about you." He stepped back to study her. "They treating you okay?"

"I can handle myself," she said. He searched her face and continued to look concerned. "They're treating me well. Really." She smiled up at him.

"How about you?" she asked, taking note of her friend's filthy clothing. She ran a finger over the fresh bruise on his cheek.

"Reasonably well," he admitted. "It's strange. They feed us, treat us decent, but keep us in the dark about their plans. None of the prisoners know why we're here or what they want with us. You're certainly the only woman prisoner I know of," he observed. He studied her, his soft, brown eyes questioning if she was telling him the full truth.

She blushed and looked at the ground. "He doesn't touch me," she said, meeting his eyes and wondering why her tone held a hint of disappointment. "Besides," she laughed, "if he does try anything, I have this." She lifted the leather folds of her skirt, revealing the knife.

Talon laughed. His eyes crinkled in fond reminiscence. "I love that you still carry that."

The knife had been a gift from him when they were teenagers. He'd had the wooden handle engraved with her initials. He pulled her in for another hug, giving her ponytail an affectionate tug.

"Break it up," Stryker said, coming up on the pair. Eyeing Talon he said, "You there, what's your name?"

"Talon."

"Talon, come with me. I've got a job for you."

Rosalie's childhood friend cast a wary look in her direction before he was led away. Saddened at losing his company so quickly, she trudged back to her room.

Ash was in the bedroom when she returned. He stood, brooding in the corner. When she shut the door, he walked towards her. His confident gait made him both sexy and dangerous and she bit down hard on her lip.

When he stood before her, he placed a hand on her leg, just below the hem of her skirt. He gazed into her eyes, and she stared back with intensity, challenging him. She hated herself for wanting him the way she did. Her breathing hitched and her pulse quickened whenever he got close.

She closed her eyes and shivered with pleasure as he slid his hand to her inner thigh. She waited for the moment he'd realize she was naked beneath the strips of leather. But to her surprise, he grabbed hold of the sheath that held the knife and jerked her forward. Her eyes snapped open.

"I know you carry this, just so you know," he said. She tensed and braced herself for a fight, squaring her shoulders and clenching her fists at her sides. "Hey, take it easy," Ash said, taking a step back and allowing Rosalie some room. He had been trying to make a point, but he hadn't intended to frighten her. Unless it proved necessary, he didn't believe in using his size or position to intimidate someone smaller than him. "Look, I know you need it to feel safe, which is why I'm allowing it."

"Thank you," she said softly, relaxing her shoulders. She lowered her eyes to the floor.

Ash stepped towards her again and tipped her chin upward.

Keep your head up. Never look down. Rosalie's father's words echoed in her ears as she fought back tears.

Several tendrils of her hair had escaped her ponytail and Ash gently pushed them out of her face. His hands lingered on her face then moved down to her shoulders, holding her captive as he gazed into her eyes. "You don't need it with me, okay, but I get why you'd want it." He breathed a heavy, tortured sigh. "Just don't make me regret letting you keep it." Without another word, he released her and walked out of the room, leaving her trembling all over.

By the time she collected herself and left the room again, most of the men had left to invade the isolated village of Talkina. She felt guilty. Perhaps she should have done more to stop it. She also felt anxious. What would happen if the gas didn't work and the villagers fought back? She shivered at the thought.

A small group of people were left behind. One man stood guard outside her room but didn't stop her when she made her way to the outer courtyard being used as a makeshift stable area for the horses. She was pleased to find a woman amongst the group. She didn't recall noticing her before. She made her way over to where the short, heavyset woman stood brushing out a beautiful, painted mare.

"I'm Rosalie," she introduced herself.

The brown-haired woman looked up and smiled but didn't say anything.

"I was brought in from Mabel Village," she continued.

A nod of acknowledgement, but still silence.

"How long have you been here?"

The woman continued to brush the painted mare. She bobbed her head from side to side, as if humming a tune, but no sound came out. Rosalie stared back at her in confusion.

"She's deaf and mute," a man's voice spoke up from behind her.

She turned to see a young man approaching, carrying a feeding bucket. He was neatly dressed, and his black hair was slicked straight back. He was of slight build and looked no more than twenty. Rosalie noticed he walked with a slight limp that he tried to conceal.

"What happened to her?" She couldn't help but pry.

"Nobody knows. She wasn't always like this. It happened shortly after Ash picked her up from Scandindale. Some say she was lovestruck."

Rosalie narrowed her eyes. Then the woman and young man burst into laughter and she realized they were messing with her. She turned away in exasperation, but the woman called after her.

"Wait, sorry. We were just having a little fun with you. Come back."

Turning back around, Rosalie softened her glare. She didn't like to be made the fool, but she missed companionship. "You got me," she smiled.

"How many times we played that trick, Leithys?"

The young man grinned. "Countless times. Since I was about four." He chuckled to himself as he limped away to complete his chores.

"That's my baby brother," the woman explained, smiling broadly. "He's not much of a fighter but he's wonderful with the animals and a hard worker."

Rosalie smiled back. "May I help?" she asked, motioning towards the horses. She'd always admired horses – though she'd never owned one herself.

"Be my guest," the woman said, handing her a brush. "My name's Othelia."

"Pleased to meet you. Do you mind if I ask a personal question?"

"Why am I the only woman in the camp?" she said, anticipating the question.

Rosalie smiled at her. "Is it such an obvious question?"

"Would be if I was in your shoes." Othelia frowned, apologetically. "It was thought the men would be too distracted by women in the camp. Most women were happy to stay back and keep the home fires burning. That wasn't an option for me. Leithys wanted to come – and I'm here to look after Leithys. Been doing it my whole life. They made an exception for me."

"Nice of them," Rosalie said sarcastically.

"They probably figured I was too fat to get the menfolk excited."

"Not true!" Rosalie said. "I mean, I was pretty excited when I saw you," she said with a wink.

Othelia snorted with laughter.

The women fell into comfortable silence as they turned their focus to brushing the tethered horses. The only break in the quiet was when Othelia offered grooming tips. Rosalie hummed softly to herself as she worked, captivity temporarily forgotten. Amongst the company of horses and her newfound friend, she was at peace.

CHAPTER SIX

When the men returned from Talkina, Rosalie was on edge. She wanted to ask if there were any casualties. She wanted to ask if they'd taken prisoners. Instead, she avoided Ash altogether and volunteered to help Othelia prepare dinner.

"Can you cook?" her friend teased.

"I do alright." She figured she couldn't do any worse than the food she'd been served lately, but she kept the sentiment to herself. She got the feeling Othelia might have prepared it.

The hostel had a generous-sized kitchen. Much of the cookware had been looted, and what remained was in poor shape, but the two women managed to find a couple decent-sized pots. They chopped up vegetables and browned the daulket meat, freshly killed that morning.

"Who does the hunting?" Rosalie asked. She enjoyed hunting daulket. The magnificent bird, with its large wingspan and aggressive personality, was always a welcome challenge.

"It depends," Othelia said as she stirred the broth. "We all take turns."

"You hunt too?" Her eyes gleamed at the exciting prospect of hunting with her new friend.

"Mostly spear hunting. Bullets are in short supply, and my rifle aim isn't so hot."

Rosalie smiled broadly. "I love spear hunting. I was a huntress in my village." She clamped her mouth shut, fearing she'd revealed too much. She was proud of being a skilled huntress. She'd used her talents to keep herself fed and to make a modest living off selling the meat and skins she hadn't needed for herself. But Ash still believed her attire marked her as a warrior.

Othelia noticed her clam up. Smiling warmly, she said, "I'll put in a good word for you. Perhaps we can take you hunting one of these mornings."

Allowing herself to relax again, Rosalie smiled back. "I'd like that very much."

At dinner everyone gathered around the campfire, swapping stories and singing old bar tunes. The fact they were in good spirits gave Rosalie hope things had gone well. She scanned the faces of the men for Stryker and Ash, but they were nowhere to be seen. *Counting the spoils of their victory*, she thought bitterly.

She also learned the prisoners would be served the warm meal she and Othelia had prepared. The detainees weren't allowed to join the rest of the men, but their needs hadn't been forgotten. Rosalie offered to take dinner to them, but her request was denied.

Once dinner was over, and dishes scrubbed clean, she searched for further excuses to keep herself busy. She learned the hostel contained a laundry room tucked behind the main office. She gathered up bags of dirty clothes from the men, including the prisoners, and headed to the laundry room. When Othelia offered to help, Rosalie politely told her she wanted to be alone. While she waited for the loads to finish, she went over in her head how she would broach the conversation with Ash about how the raid had gone. He was under no obligation to tell her, but something inside her told her he would. Perhaps that's what scared her — that he would be too truthful if things hadn't gone well.

Hours later, when the laundry was washed, dried, and folded, she couldn't avoid Ash any longer. After making the rounds to deliver the clean clothes, she made her way back to their shared room. She found herself conflicted about seeing him, fearing what he might reveal. But above that fear, she felt longing. She missed him. She could scarcely contain her excitement as she quickened her pace.

Not sure why, she knocked on the door to room 4 and waited for a response. Ash opened the door to her, shirtless and barefoot. He stepped to the side and invited her in. She entered, and when he closed the door, she stood awkward before him.

A thousand questions fired off in her brain, each one related to the raid on Talkina and how it had gone. "How are you?" she asked instead.

He gazed back at her, knowing what she wanted to ask. "No casualties. It went as planned."

She nodded, relieved. "And your new prisoners?"

There was a pause. "We took three new recruits."

Rosalie snorted at his choice of words.

He sighed wearily. "Is this going to be a fight?"

"No," she said, averting her eyes. "I don't want it to be. I just don't understand."

"Someday you will," he told her. But it's all he offered up.

It was getting late, and there was no avoiding the subject of the single bed. "I'm willing to share," she spoke bravely. Her gaze traveled up and down his bare, muscular chest before resting on his clear blue eyes.

Ash hesitated, pretending to mull it over for the first time. If he was being honest, he'd been thinking about the single bed since they'd first arrived.

Heart pounding, she thought of offering for him to tie her up but worried it would give him the wrong idea. *Or the right idea.*

"I will sleep on the floor," he said decidedly.

"Are you sure? I know you're struggling with your back."

He nodded. "I'll be fine. I just have to grab some extra blankets from the front office." He tugged on a shirt and shoes and headed toward the door. With one hand on the door handle, he stopped and turned to face her. "You going to be okay here?"

She knew what he meant. *Can I trust you to be here when I get back?*

"I'll be here."

Ash took his time securing the blankets. As he inventoried the office, he wondered what he was doing with Rosalie. She was important to the mission but was that enough excuse to keep her at his bedside? He already knew the answer. The woman was maddening. Intriguing. He felt an overwhelming need to protect her – yet, somehow, he knew she didn't need his protection. She was spirited and strong, and his arms ached to hold her. When he wasn't with her, she invaded his thoughts without warning. *You need to get a handle on this*, he scolded himself aloud. Problem was, he didn't know how. When it came to Rosalie, he was in uncharted waters.

Rosalie couldn't sleep. She heard Ash's restless groans from where he slept on the worn, carpeted floor. She knew he should have taken the bed, but he had to be so irritatingly chivalrous. Now they were both suffering. She crept out of bed. The floor joists flexed and creaked beneath her feet. She froze, but Ash didn't stir. She crouched beside him, her eyes adjusting to the dark. She sighed when she realized he was lying flat on his back. It would make what she planned to do much harder.

Slowly, she slid her hands underneath him, feeling around until she found the injured site in his lumbar region. Closing her eyes in concentration, she did her best to ignore the warmth she felt at being so close to him. She murmured a soft chant. As she spoke the soothing words, she felt his pain lessening. She caressed his skin and her fingers tingled as the mending began.

When both Ash's groans and the tingling sensation in her fingertips subsided, she knew the pain had left him. Satisfied, she pulled her hands free.

He stirred and grabbed her, pulling her close. She sucked in her breath in surprise as he pressed her against him.

"Ash?" she whispered, but he didn't respond.

When she realized he was still asleep, she relaxed and allowed herself to remain cradled in his arms. Unable to stop herself, she kissed his bare chest, then rested her cheek where she'd planted the kiss. Desire stirred within her as her imagination ran wild. She wanted to feel his firm hands on her skin and to experience the warmth of his mouth against her lips.

She reckoned he'd be a generous lover. Unselfish. Experienced, though she didn't want to think about the women of his past who had shared his bed. She pushed them out of her mind and let herself lay there longer than she should. Finally, body and mind tormented with unfulfilled longing she could no longer endure, she disentangled herself from his arms and snuck back into bed.

CHAPTER SEVEN

"My back feels amazing," Ash told Rosalie the next morning. He wore a peculiar smile.

"Sounds like you're healing up," she suggested. She bit the inside of her lip to stifle a grin.

He stared up at her from where he remained stretched out on the floor. "I had the strangest dream last night." There was a glint of amusement in his eyes and Rosalie felt her cheeks flush.

Still feigning innocence, she replied, "Really? I slept like a rock." Unable to meet his gaze, she climbed out of bed and headed for the bathroom. "Glad you're feeling better," she called over her shoulder. She discarded her clothes on the bathroom floor and stepped into the shower, bracing herself for the frigid water.

When the water hit her skin, she jumped out of the shower and ran naked back into the bedroom like her hair was on fire. She was shouting excitedly.

Ash leapt to his feet. "What's wrong?"

"Hot water. We have hot water!"

He chuckled and did his best to keep his eyes from exploring her naked form. "Yeah, they got that fixed last night."

"And you didn't tell me?" She slapped him playfully on the arm. "My day has just been made. I don't think you understand." She ran back to the bathroom to bask in the warmth of the steamy water.

Ash stared after her bare backside as she scampered away, then he sat on the edge of the bed and decided his shower would need to be cold. The woman really didn't have a shred of modesty.

Rosalie sat down to breakfast by herself. Most of the camp had eaten and when she'd left the room, Ash was still in the shower. As she grazed on her breakfast of hardened bread and leftover mush, she thought about her predicament. She really needed to find Talon and work out an escape plan. It was the most responsible, rational thing to do. But whenever she was with Ash, somehow escape didn't feel like a priority.

"Speaking of hot water," Ash spoke up behind her, interrupting her thoughts. This time she didn't jump at his unexpected presence and it pleased him. He sat beside her and handed her a steaming mug. "Krisha tea," he said.

"What? Really!" His hair was still wet from the shower and her heart skipped a beat at seeing the seductive way his wayward locks clung to his forehead. She curled her fingers around the warm mug and told herself it was the tea that had her heart pounding. The familiar, spicy scent of the tea filled her with longing and nostalgia. She closed her eyes as she took her first sip, pausing before she swallowed so she could savor the bold flavors. She'd been missing krisha tea since leaving Mabel

Village. It was a rare luxury for most; something to be cherished. She had been fortunate to enjoy it in abundance since childhood.

Her family had harvested the krisha tea leaves in their small garden. When her parents moved away, they'd left her an abundant supply of the leaves, and a few plants to care for on her own. She'd previously relied on her mother's gardening talents, which were far superior to her own; but her desire to drink krisha tea whenever she wished forced her to step up her game. She'd soon become an expert gardener, tending to the delicate plants daily. *They are probably wilted beyond repair now*, she thought sadly.

"How did you know?" She turned to him, amazed.

Ash shrugged but she caught the grin he tried to mask behind his feigned indifference.

What he didn't tell her was he indirectly had Talon to thank for the information. His inside man had a talent for gaining the trust of the prisoners and getting them to talk openly; and Talon loved to talk about Rosalie and the life they had back home. To Ash's relief, it didn't appear the two were lovers, though he wondered if they had a past Talon was too much of a gentleman to share.

"Thank you." Her eyes flitted to his, then back to her tea.

When his eyes met hers, he had a vision of her closing her eyes and pressing her luscious lips to his; murmuring in appreciation the way she'd done as she took her first sip of tea. Annoyed with himself and the realization the cold shower hadn't worked to wrangle his errant thoughts into submission, he shrugged off the fantasy and stood to his feet. "I have to take care of some things," he muttered sharply, stalking away.

Rosalie took another sip of her tea and wondered to herself what she'd done to alter his mood so quickly.

After Ash left that morning, Rosalie made up her mind to find Talon. It might be difficult, but she could be sneaky when she needed to be. She opened the door, not surprised to see a man waiting on the other side. "Bentli, right?"

The short, heavyset man grunted in response.

"I was going to find Othelia and see if she needed any help."

"Othelia went to the village."

The simple sentence was like a punch to her gut. She couldn't bear the thought of her new friend looting homes and taking people against their will. Anger and frustration stirred within her.

"Okay," she said, trying to appear unphased. "Then I think I'll see what laundry needs to be done." She'd trained the men to drop off their soiled clothes in the laundry room; even taught them how to separate them into proper piles. Darks, lights; leathers and furs.

"I'll go with you."

"I can take care of myself," she said, trying to keep her tone light and friendly.

"I have no doubts that you can," he said, his tone equally friendly. But he fell into step beside her. She felt flustered but was determined to get the best of him. A few hours of boredom in the laundry room ought to do him in.

Rosalie's assumption was correct. By her second round of laundry, Bentli's interest was fading. "I'm going to check in on a few things," he announced. Pretending to be content folding clothes, she shrugged as if it didn't matter to her whether he stayed with her.

"I'll be back." His voice held a warning.

"See you in a bit." She flashed a wink and a smile, then returned her attention to the laundry.

Bentli paused a moment longer, shifting from one pudgy foot to another. Then, seeming to decide she would remain put, he left the room.

She waited for the appropriate amount of time to pass before she slipped out of the laundry room. She headed in the direction she knew the prisoners were being held – the backside of the hostel. She was close to her destination when she heard a familiar voice behind her.

"I figured you couldn't be trusted."

She jumped, then turned to face Ash. Her throat tightened and her spine tingled – an exhilarating blend of fear and anticipation she often felt when she was near him. Her mind raced for an excuse to explain what she was up to. But to her surprise, when she caught his gaze, his expression was one of amusement rather than anger.

"I'm sorry," she said, biting her lip nervously. "I just wanted to be sure Talon was alright."

"He's fine." He kept his tone reassuring, but short.

"Don't be mad," she pleaded, eyes watering. She wasn't afraid of him, she decided. Her greatest fear at that moment was disappointing him.

He exhaled slowly as he stared back at her, studying her obvious discomfort. He found her adorable when she was nervous. Gods help him, he found her adorable no matter how she was. He cocked his head ever so slightly and his blue eyes softened. "I'm not mad. I understand why you'd want to check on your friend. I promise you, he's fine."

Her shoulders relaxed and Ash could see the relief wash across her face.

"Back so soon?" she asked, desperate to change the subject.

"Just a quick supply run," he explained. He looked beyond tired. He looked drained, like something was weighing heavy on his conscience, and Rosalie wanted to reach out to him. She stepped towards him and touched his cheek. He leaned into her hand, then took it in his and pressed it to his lips.

Her body warmed with desire as she imagined how his lips would feel against hers. She knew it was pointless to deny how she felt. She wanted him. Mind made up, she asked in a sultry voice, "Should we go back to our room?"

Ash stared back at her. His face clouded in confusion, but he fell into step beside her.

Rosalie's heart thudded in her chest as she led the way back to room 4. Once inside, she locked the door so they wouldn't be disturbed. She checked that the curtains were secure before she moved towards him, pressing herself against him. She stood on her tiptoes and kissed his cheek, then his lips.

At first, Ash was taken back. He knew he should push her away, but instead he found himself lengthening the kiss. His conscience took flight and his breathing became erratic. He unbuttoned her blouse. Her lacy, black bra fastened in the front and he unhooked it with one hand, freeing her breasts. She gasped as he pushed her shirt and bra straps off her shoulders and caressed her skin. She basked in his warmth and marveled at his experienced hands. They were large, callused, and every touch made her shiver with pleasure.

"Are you sure about this?" he asked.

Rosalie nodded.

"If you're doing this because you're afraid of me…"

"I'm not afraid of you." Her eyes were ablaze with passion.

He leaned in to kiss her again, but then stopped himself. "I'm sorry, I can't." He backed away from her.

"Why not?" she asked, her cheeks warming with the sting of rejection. She could feel her throat tighten as her confidence faltered.

"Rosalie, you are beautiful. I want you. Maybe more than I've ever wanted anything. But you're my prisoner. It would be wrong. I'd be taking advantage."

"I'm *asking* you to take advantage of me." She hesitated, then took a step closer.

He smiled and the corners of his eyes crinkled. "Believe me, you have no idea how bad I want to." He wrestled with his desires as he fought to remain strong against her; for her. "But I promise you, it's not going to gain you your freedom. It's not going to alter my actions or make me return you or anything else to your village. My mission is firm. It goes beyond the desire I have for you."

She nodded. "I understand. I do."

He gazed at her, longingly. Slowly, tenderly, he traced her jawline with his fingertips, then tipped her chin upwards. His eyes bore into hers. "But if things were different…"

"I wasn't finished," she interrupted. Her green, almond-shaped eyes burned. "I understand what you're saying. And knowing that, I still want you."

"Roe."

He sounded pained and she shuddered with pleasure as the intimate nickname rolled off his tongue. "Please don't make me beg," she whispered.

"I can't..."

"Please," she said hoarsely. "I know it won't change anything. And I can't explain the way I feel, but I'm fairly certain if you don't make love to me right now, I may never forgive you." A single tear escaped and ran down her cheek, surprising them both.

Ash reached up to wipe away the tear with his thumb and Rosalie's hand closed over his. She moved his hand downward, letting it rest on her exposed bosom. Her breasts were small, but firm, and his heartrate spiked. He gave up trying to be chivalrous. He tore the shirt and bra from her body and ran his teeth over each nipple. "Tell me again you want me," he growled. He needed to hear it – needed to be sure.

"I want all of you," she panted as her hands loosened his belt buckle and she yanked down his pants. "Please, Ash. Make love to me."

He knew she might hate him in the morning; maybe he'd hate himself. But he could no longer resist her pleas. He kicked out of his pants and briefs before returning his focus to her. He removed her leather skirt and tossed it in the corner. She wasn't wearing panties, a fact that pleased him but somehow didn't come as a shock. Rosalie shivered as he untied the sheathed knife from her thigh.

Naked, they fell together onto the bed, lost in each other. Ash's lips claimed her throat, then her mouth. His fingers found the folds of her womanhood and he slid his fingers inside her. She bucked wildly in anticipation. "Ash," she cried out as he tormented her with his hands. Her fingernails dug into his back and she pulled him closer. He wasn't her first, but her body writhed with impatience and desire as if it was her first time.

"You ready?" he asked. He was hard and ached to feel her.

When she nodded, he slid his way inside her. His need was intense, and his movements were greedy and rough. Rosalie didn't mind. She needed to feel all of him. Weeks of frustration built up inside her and she longed to feel his punishing thrusts.

"Is this what you needed, Roe?" he asked wickedly, brushing his lips across her ear.

In response, she lifted her hips and met his urgent rhythm.

When it was over, they both lay panting. Rosalie braced herself for Ash to announce he was going to sleep on the floor, but he snuggled up to her instead, pulling her into his arms so her head rested on his torso. She smiled with satisfaction. She could hear the pounding in his chest and his labored breathing in response to their lovemaking.

He kissed the top of her head and held her tight, draping one leg over hers. Perhaps he thought she would try to escape, but she had no intention of doing so. She felt confounding contentment in the arms of her captor.

When morning came, Rosalie was pleased to discover Ash was still in bed with her. She awoke nestled in his arms. She sighed and moved in closer, feeling the swell of him beside her. "I gather you're awake."

Ash chuckled. "I've been lying here thinking about all the ways I could take advantage of you while you slept." But she knew he was teasing. Despite giving into her, he was too honorable a man to do any such thing.

A long pause followed as she considered where they would go from there.

"You okay about last night?" he asked, breaking the silence. He would only feel regret if she did. Moments stretched into eternity as he waited for her answer.

"Last night," she finally said, "you called me Roe."

"And?"

"Only my friends call me Roe."

She sat up in bed and stared over at him. He smoothed her hair and held her intense gaze. "I heard Talon call you that. I liked it. It suits you. Is it okay if I call you Roe?"

She paused to consider. She loved to hear it on his lips. But it felt so intimate, and she didn't want to confuse her feelings for him. Despite her worries, she found herself saying, "Yes."

She laid her head back on his chest. He stroked her hair. Neither wanted to move. Ash worried he'd been too rough with her, but her body language suggested otherwise. His desire stirred as he remembered the way she'd given into her hunger and begged for her release. His fingers trailed to her bare buttocks, then up her side. She squirmed.

"Are you ticklish?"

"Very."

When he stroked her side again, she giggled and tried to escape his touch. Her laugh was care-free. It was the first time he had heard it. He reached out and touched her face. His thumb traced her lips. "I love your laugh," he admitted.

His hypnotic blue eyes drew her to him. She found herself leaning in to kiss him. Her eyes closed, and her lips parted as they met his. He swept his tongue inside her mouth and she whimpered with pleasure.

This time, when Ash entered her, his movements were slow and careful. He wanted to make the moment last. He wanted to hear Rosalie moan with longing and appreciation as he took his time with her. "You're so beautiful, Roe," he whispered.

She smiled up at him, then closed her eyes and let herself get lost in his movements. She matched his careful rhythm, all the while pretending he was hers to keep. Her worries from before resurfaced, but she knew it was too late. Her judgement was already clouded. She was already lost in her feelings for him.

CHAPTER EIGHT

"You seem off today," Stryker observed. The small army had been riding for over an hour towards the village of Bachtoy, and while Ash would normally keep everyone's spirits high with stories of past victories, or tales from his rebellious youth, today he was unusually quiet.

"How so?" Ash straightened in the saddle and focused on the road ahead.

"I mean you are wearing a stupid grin and appear to have an entirely different conquest on your mind."

Ash's smile faded in response to Stryker's innuendo and was replaced by a look of determination. "I assure you I am only thinking of *this* mission."

"Uh huh. Did you finally take her?"

Ash's hands tightened on the reins. He turned to face his friend. "It's not like that."

"Then what's it like? C'mon, spill. The rest of us have to face the cool nights alone. The least you can do is tell us how she tastes."

Without warning, Ash made a fist and busted Stryker in the teeth.

Startled, he fell off his horse, landing hard on the rough terrain below. His right arm bore the brunt of the fall. "You hit me!" he bellowed, scrambling to his feet and wiping the blood from his mouth.

In an instant Ash was off his horse and the two men stood toe to toe. "I won't permit you to talk about her that way."

"Oh, you won't permit me?" Stryker swung hard, but Ash ducked his swing and landed a punch to Stryker's midsection. His knees buckled at the blow. "I'll kill you," he screamed. He tackled Ash at the knees and the two men fell to the ground. They rolled around thrashing until Ash tossed Stryker off him and stood to his feet. Stryker stood, brushing the dirt from his pantlegs. He lunged at Ash once more.

"Easy. Easy." Stryker's brother, Dillinger, stepped in between the two men, nearly taking an elbow to his eye for his troubles. "You two are friends. Are you really going to risk that for some woman?"

When Ash started to apologize, Stryker shoved him hard. "Some of us would, I guess." Disgusted, he turned back to his horse.

Narrowing his eyes, Dillinger turned accusingly towards Ash, who mumbled something under his breath. "We done here?" Dillinger asked. "Because last I checked, we had a mission to accomplish."

Ash looked around at the army of men. Many had dismounted and were standing around nervously. All eyes were on him. "We're done. Now everyone can stop gawking. Mount up and let's move."

Stryker rode out ahead, Dillinger by his side, and Ash directly behind them. "We may want to call off the raid today if everyone's head isn't in the game," Dillinger told Stryker, but loud enough for Ash to hear.

Ash nudged his horse forward, coming up beside the two men. He glanced over at them and grunted. "Let Stryker worry about his own pretty head. Mine's just fine." His face broke into a mischievous grin.

Dillinger laughed.

"What's so funny?" Stryker barked.

"Well, you are sort of pretty," his brother teased.

Ash laughed too, a deep, boisterous laugh that started in his belly.

Despite his efforts to remain angry, a smile tugged at the corner of Stryker's mouth. "Ain't many people accused me of being pretty. Especially another man."

Ash slapped his friend on the back. "Don't get too used to it."

Both men knew it was the closest either would come to an apology.

"I brought you something," Ash told Rosalie when he returned. From behind his back he produced a lumpy package wrapped in brown paper. He was grinning, clearly pleased with himself – but he appeared apprehensive to what her reaction might be.

She wanted to ask if he'd stolen it from one of the villages, but she didn't want to dampen his mood. She hesitated before taking the package.

"I bought it at a little store just outside of town," he explained.

Rosalie's ears turned pink and she wondered if it had been that obvious, what she was thinking. Ash was smiling, so she smiled back at him as she carefully opened the wrinkled packaging.

Inside was a hairbrush, two pairs of pants, three shirts, and several pairs of panties. Nothing fancy, but everything looked roughly her size. "New clothes," she said, surprised.

"I thought you could use some clothes that fit."

She grinned widely, then hugged him. "Thank you. You don't know what this means to me."

"Well, really it's for me," he teased. "Your clothes are not warm enough for the changing season – not to mention being scandalously short – and I've grown a bit tired of seeing you in those drab, used clothes I gave you."

She shoved him playfully. "I thought I was pulling them off just fine."

He kissed her softly on the mouth. "I suppose you were."

CHAPTER NINE

Rosalie propped an elbow on the pillow and supported her head in her hand. She gazed over at Ash and pondered the man she saw before her. The man whose bed she'd been sharing for the past several nights and whom she still knew so little about.

"What do you like?" she finally asked.

"What do you mean?" He stared back at her, wearing a puzzled expression.

"I mean, what do you like? What do you do for fun? You know, when you're not conquering villages and dragging women back to your lair."

A flicker of sadness shadowed his handsome face, but he recovered quickly and flashed a broad smile.

"I like this," he said, skimming his index finger over her bare thigh.

She shivered with pleasure at the way his touch spread warmth over her body. "What else? Dig deeper."

He paused and closed his eyes, gathering his thoughts. Then he opened them again and grinned back at her. "I like grilled cheese sandwiches," he said playfully as he planted a kiss on her chin. She squealed with delight. "I like riding bareback through the rain." His mouth found hers and her lips responded, drinking him in.

"Go on," she said, coming up for air.

"Hmm. Back home, when I had a home, I liked playing cards with friends." He continued to smile, but sadness once again marred his features.

"So, if I rode up bareback on a horse, holding a grilled cheese sandwich and a deck of cards?"

He chuckled. "I might like you too."

"Dang, you're a hard man to please," she teased. She pulled him towards her.

"I think I like you even without the sandwich," he said softly as he placed a kiss on the tip of her nose. This time it was her turn to be sad. She had fallen harder than she was willing to admit – especially to herself.

"What's wrong?"

"Nothing, just thinking."

"About?"

Silence followed as a thousand thoughts and insecurities bounced around in her head.

"When you grow tired of me, would you ever pass me off?" she finally blurted out.

Ash wanted to laugh but noticed Rosalie's unsmiling face. "Is that seriously what you think of me?" He'd feel insulted if he wasn't so surprised.

"Well, not necessarily, but then again, I really don't know you."

"I'd say you know me more intimately than most." He flashed her a wicked grin and gave her hair a playful tug.

"Would you?" she asked again. Her cheeks burned. "I mean, what if your leader wanted to…" Her voice trailed off and she shivered at the thought.

"Roe, I give you my word, no one else will touch you," he told her. "Besides, I don't plan to tire of you." He nipped at her shoulder and rolled her over onto her stomach. She squealed as he smothered her backside in kisses and slapped her playfully on the rear. When his fingers touched the scar on her shoulder blade, she tensed.

"How did you get this?"

"Ugly, right?"

"No, Love. Nothing about you is ugly. I was just curious." She felt the warmth of his mouth on her marred skin.

"I don't want to talk about it," she admitted. "Brings up too many painful memories." She rolled onto her back and gazed up at him. Her cheeks were pink, and her eyes misted. "Is that okay?"

He touched her warm cheek and leaned in close. "You don't have to share anything you don't want to," he assured her. "But I'm here if there is anything you'd like to."

His words were gentle, but they stabbed at her heart. They made her care about him; and she didn't want to care. She knew it couldn't end well for them. They each had their own mission to accomplish. And their missions, whether Ash realized it or not, were headed in different directions.

When Ash slipped out of his room that evening under the cover of night, Stryker was already waiting for him on the other side of the door.

"Ready?" Stryker asked.

Ash secured a stocking cap on his head, tugging it over his hair and ears. "As ready as I'll ever be. Do you think anything's changed?" The hope in his voice was fading and Stryker didn't respond.

Cloaked by the darkness, the pair walked in silence towards the secluded room in the back of the hostel, using the dimly lit walkways as a guide. The night air was chilling – evidence the clement season was coming to a close. Ash shoved his hands into his pants pockets and marveled at the way Stryker appeared unaffected by the bitter cold.

"Really, you're not the least bit cold?" he finally asked. His fingertips felt like icicles and his breath froze as it passed his lips.

Stryker laughed. "It's not even the harvest season yet. You've been hanging out with women too long."

His tone was good-natured, but Ash detected a trace of judgement. He felt a surge of warmth as he thought of Rosalie. "We need her," he defended.

"Some of us more than others," Stryker mumbled. He stopped midstride and gave Ash a pointed look.

"I know what I'm doing."

"Hmph."

Silence. Then Stryker said, "Hey, do you remember when we were kids, and we went to that party in Old Man Kitsyn's barn?"

"Yes." He wondered where Stryker was going with this.

"And remember Himney had stolen his dad's stash of chewing tobacco?"

"Yes." His eyes twinkled as he recalled that evening with fondness.

"And as good as the chewing tobacco smelled, and regardless of the street cred it would have given me, you warned me not to try it. Told me that the consequences would outweigh the thrill."

Ash stopped and looked at his friend, realizing too late where this was headed.

Stryker continued. "Of course, I didn't listen. I couldn't resist a taste. I'll never forget that first tingling sensation when I put the tobacco in my mouth... Ended up losing my dinner over the railing of the loft and all down my shirt."

Ash laughed but Stryker's expression turned sober. He placed a meaty hand on Ash's shoulder and looked him square in the eye. "No matter how enticing, sometimes the taste isn't worth the aftermath."

Lost for a response, Ash cleared his throat, then turned and knocked on the door to room 22 instead. He knew the man behind the door would validate his decision to keep Rosalie as a hostage. How he'd chosen to go about it might be another matter.

When Marx answered the door, he motioned for the two men to enter. After looking around to ensure no one followed them, he closed the door and secured it behind him. Tonight, over beers, there was much to discuss.

"I know that wasn't the news you were hoping for," Stryker said once the two friends were back outside.

Ash nodded. "It is what it is. It's still good news for the cause. Sometimes sacrifices have to be made."

Stryker nodded, but he doubted his friend fully believed the words he'd just spoken. He patted his pocket and pulled out a bitterroot cig.

Ash gave him a sideways look.

"Relax," he said, holding up the cig. "This isn't another metaphor." He lit the cig, took a drag, then closed his eyes. "You know, I had my first taste of bitterroot when I was 12? I've had a love/hate relationship with it ever since."

"Smells disgusting," Ash told him. "Never touched the stuff."

Stryker chuckled and patted his pocket again for more. "My friend, you don't know what you're missing."

Ash grunted. He knew what he was missing. And it wasn't the bitterroot. On the way back to his room, he wrestled with his conscience until he landed on a decision. It wasn't fair to Rosalie to lead her on when he knew the outcome. Without intending to, he'd blurred the lines between her captor and her lover. He needed to back off.

CHAPTER TEN

Ash could tell his indifference towards Rosalie was having an impact. More than once he caught the hurt in her eyes when he cold-shouldered her. From the start of the day until now, he hadn't touched her. No morning kiss, no casual holding of her hand. He already missed it.

At dinner he'd fought the urge to tuck a stray strand of her hair behind her ear. He'd clutched his fork instead and kept his eyes trained on his food.

"I might go stay with Othelia tonight," Rosalie announced once dinner was over.

The announcement caught him by surprise. "Why?"

Her eyes glistened with tears – tears he could tell she was fighting to hold back. "I think we could probably use a break from each other." She forced a smile. It slayed him. He didn't want to cause her pain.

"I'd like you to stay."

"Would you?" Her eyes misted as she searched his for an honest answer.

He nodded but didn't say more. He ached to hold her but told himself he needed to stand firm. After all, he was doing the right thing. *Wasn't he?*

While Rosalie was busy getting ready for bed, Ash slipped out of the room to take a walk and clear the regret clouding his decision. As he passed by the dying campfire, he recalled how beautiful Rosalie looked in the glow of the flames. He'd seen the way other men gawked at her from across the campfire, but she'd never seemed to notice.

He walked towards the stables. As he stopped in to check on the horses, he thought about the way her eyes lit up when she was around them; and how she'd won over Othelia, which was not an easy feat. Circling the laundry room, he was haunted by the memory of that first night she'd asked him to make love to her. He took one last walk around the perimeter of the camp then headed back to his room.

When he opened the door, he saw Rosalie was already asleep. He stripped off his clothes and slipped into bed beside her, pulling her close and molding his body against hers. The scent of jasmine lingered in the air. He'd changed his mind. He couldn't ignore her. He was going to try in every way to show her how much he cared about her. And he was going to do everything in his power to change the fate Marx had foreseen for her.

CHAPTER ELEVEN

Ash nudged Rosalie awake before the rise of the morning sun. She stirred, murmured her displeasure of the early hour, and turned her back to him, facing the wall. She squeezed her eyes shut, blocking out the pain of his indifference the day before. She wondered how she'd face it another day. She'd fallen asleep thinking about it, dreamt about it, but the new day hadn't brought the answers she'd been seeking.

"I want to show you something, Roe," Ash spoke up softly beside her. He skimmed his index finger over her shoulder and down her bare back. She did her best not to shiver at his touch.

"Wake up, my beauty," he tried again. She smiled to herself, still facing the wall. Ash leaned down, swept her hair out of her face, and placed a kiss on her cheek. He thought he tasted the salt of her tears. It left a dull ache inside him.

"I want to show you something," he repeated. "Will you come with me? You have to be very quiet though."

She turned to face him, nodded, but her face was void of emotion. He kissed her chin, then climbed out of bed and headed toward the dresser. Rosalie stared after his naked backside as he crossed the room. From the top dresser drawer, he produced two, thin robes. "Put this on," he said, handing Rosalie one of the robes.

She looked at him in confusion. "Shouldn't I get dressed?"

"Not where we're going," he said, giving her a lopsided grin.

She climbed out of bed. Ash admired her naked frame as she slipped on the robe. He put on the second robe, then took her by the hand. The pair crept to the window and peeked through the curtains. The man tasked with guarding the door was snoring softly in his chair.

"Volunteers," Ash smirked. He eased the door open with care, putting his index finger to his lips to warn Rosalie to keep quiet. She rolled her eyes but smiled back at him. They crept past the guard and towards the back of the hostel. All the while Ash held Rosalie's hand firmly in his. When they reached the backside of the inn, he pointed in the direction of the tree line just beyond the camp. Sun still asleep, Rosalie could barely see the outline of the trees against the darkened sky.

"We're headed in that direction. You up for it?"

There was a chill in the air and she pulled her robe tighter. She nodded. Her heart pounded and her brain fired off mixed emotions. She felt exhilaration at the prospect of a shared adventure, the danger of being caught, and above all, uncertainty and confusion at his changed treatment of her. She let her hand rest in his as they raced towards the cover of the trees.

Ash led her through the forest until they reached a clearing. Beyond the clearing was a small lake. Bigger than a pond, but not by much. Steam rose from the water as it bubbled and churned. Ivy vines with brilliant, white flowers grew wild, lining the perimeter of the lake and shining like stars against the gray sky. The night larks sang softly from the brush; a low, melancholy call.

"It's breathtaking," Rosalie said. She turned to look at Ash, who was shedding his robe. "What are you doing?"

"Going for a swim."

"You'll freeze."

"Trust me," he said, winking in her direction. Then he ran towards the bubbling water, and dove in.

Rosalie stared after him. When he didn't resurface, she called out his name. Maybe he'd hit his head. Or perhaps the chill of the water had sent him into shock. This could be it, she realized; her moment of escape. She could run away under the cover of night. With her huntress skills, she was certain she could survive. But something kept her from leaving.

In a matter of seconds, she began to rationalize why she couldn't leave. She couldn't abandon Ash if he was in trouble, could she? And what about Talon? Surely, she shouldn't go without him.

No, she decided, she couldn't run. Instead, hair on her neck prickling with fear, she stripped off her own robe, ran towards the water's edge, and dove in head-first after him.

To her surprise, the water was warm. It felt like a soothing bath. When she popped her head up for air, she saw Ash bobbing above the surface, laughing.

"You scared me!" she scolded.

"But you were so cute jumping in to rescue me."

She splashed water in his direction. He ducked beneath the surface to avoid it, then popped back up.

"The water's so warm," she said, surprised.

"Yeah, it's a fire lake. Something below the surface keeps it warm year-round."

"I've read about those. Never found one though. They're rare, I hear."

"I rather like rare, beautiful things," Ash said, swimming up beside her and brushing his naked body against hers. He stroked her cheek and she leaned into his hand. "Sorry about yesterday," he told her.

He didn't offer an explanation for his actions, only an apology. Rosalie nodded, at a loss for how to respond.

"You deserve better," he told her solemnly. He cupped her chin in his hand, then leaned down and kissed her on the mouth. She wrapped her legs around him as his body formed to hers. The warmth of the water was nothing compared to the heat she felt from his presence.

When they made their way back to the camp, the sun had long since risen.

"I guess there'll be no sneaking back," Ash said. But he didn't seem concerned. He held Rosalie's hand in his as they strolled through the trees.

"Hold up," she said, pausing on the path.

"What is it?"

She strayed a short distance from the path, then knelt down next to a leafy, flowering plant. She tugged with both hands and the plant uprooted with ease. With delicate precision, she began to separate the thick, long roots from its stem.

"What are you doing?" Ash asked.

"Bitterroot," she explained.

She snapped the lengths of the roots in half, placed them in the pocket of her robe, then wiped the dirt from her hands. "I've noticed some of the men like it." What she didn't say was, she'd noticed Stryker liked it; and she hoped to present it to him as a peace offering.

Before they left the covering of the tree line, Ash stopped, turned towards Rosalie and tightened her robe around her. His own robe gaped open, exposing his chest, but she didn't try to fix it. She liked the view.

Breakfast was being set out when they arrived back at camp. Ash caught Stryker's disapproving look but chose to ignore it.

"Want breakfast?" he asked Rosalie.

She made a face. "Not if it's more of that mush."

"I think we can do better than that."

After a quick stop at their room to dress, they raided the kitchen. Rosalie cut up fruit while Ash popped bread in the toaster and rummaged through the fridge for butter.

"You need a haircut," she observed, watching the way his hair fell into his face each time he bent down.

"Yeah, well I haven't had time to find a barber."

"I could do it," she offered.

"Really?"

"Yeah, I used to cut my little brother's hair all the time. Sometimes my dad's if my mom got busy."

"Hmm..." He stroked his chin, considering.

"What, are you afraid I'll make those luscious locks too short?" she teased.

"Actually, I'm afraid of what you might do if I armed you with a sharp pair of scissors." His eyes twinkled with humor.

She held up the knife she was using to cut the fruit. "Umm... you forget I'm already armed." She shot him a wink. But as she did, the image of Talon surfaced in the back of her mind and she felt a wave of guilt at not giving the knife more consideration as a weapon. For Talon's sake.

Ash took a chair from the office and brought it to the outer courtyard. Rosalie rummaged through the kitchen drawer and managed to find a decent pair of scissors. From the front office, she grabbed an extra bath towel, a glass of water, and a comb, then joined Ash in the outer courtyard.

"Take a seat," she instructed.

He sat down, but he looked nervous.

"Oh, good grief, you *are* afraid I'll mess up that beautiful hair, aren't you?"

"Just take a little off the top," he said, looking sheepish.

She rolled her eyes, then began to work. She draped the towel over his shoulders, dipped her comb in the glass of water, then raked it through his hair. His hair was thick and silky. She let her fingers skim through it more than was necessary. She combed his hair, held a section between two fingers, then used the scissors to trim the excess length.

Ash watched the hair fall to the ground, squirmed uncomfortably, but didn't say anything.

Rosalie repeated her movements – each time letting her fingers walk through his locks and massage his scalp. After a few minutes, he relaxed and let her work.

As she was finishing up, a man wandered over and stood behind Ash's chair. Another man followed suit, positioning himself behind the first man and forming the start of a line. Rosalie grinned. "You boys want a haircut?"

They both smiled back at her and nodded.

"Okay, I'll be just a few minutes."

"All done," she told Ash once she'd finished styling his newly trimmed hair. She removed the towel from his shoulders and shook it out. "Now get a move on, we have a line."

He turned around in his chair, taking in the growing line of men. His eyebrows shot up in surprise. Begrudgingly, he got up out of his chair and offered it to the man behind him.

"She's all yours," he said. Not liking how his statement sounded, he amended, "The chair's all yours."

The man turned red. Rosalie smiled to herself, then asked the man, "How would you like it?" Ash shot her a warning look at her mocking inuendo.

Rosalie thought she was finishing up with her last customer when Stryker approached her. He didn't stand behind the chair; he stood beside it, looking impatient.

"Haircut?" she asked, her voice warbling.

He nodded.

After she finished with her current haircut, she thanked the man for his patience, then instructed Stryker to take a seat. Her fingers trembled as she combed through his blondish-white hair. "Still want this side long?" she asked timidly, referring to the side that covered the scar on his cheek. The last thing she wanted to do was offend him.

"No more than chin length."

She nodded, then got to work. She found herself unable to make the idle chitchat that came so easily with the others.

"I see you've finally found something useful to do," he said rudely.

Rosalie squeezed the scissors firmly in her hand and took a breath. "I've managed to find a few things to make myself useful." She wanted to remind him that she was the reason his meals had improved and his clothes were clean.

"Yeah, I suppose Ash could attest to that," he smirked.

Her cheeks burned and her neck tightened in anger. "That's not what I meant," she hissed.

Stryker shrugged.

She sped things up, clipping off a bigger section of hair than she normally would.

"May I remind you," she said, speaking slowly but working at a vigorous pace, "that I didn't ask to be here. Believe me, I'd rather be back home and far away from this place and all of you." As she spurted out the words, she wasn't sure how much she believed them, but she thought they got her point across.

"Finally, something we can agree on." His tone was flat; hollow.

Exasperated, Rosalie finished the haircut in silence. When she was done, she removed the towel, wiped the hair from his shoulders, then announced, "All done."

Those two words were of great comfort to her.

When Stryker stood to leave, she said, "Oh, I almost forgot. This is for you." She removed the bitterroot from her pants pocket, pressed it into his palm, then walked away; her shoulders squared with pride.

Stryker watched her saunter away. When he opened his hand to see what she'd given him, he softened a little. He exhaled slowly and felt an unfamiliar wave of shame.

CHAPTER TWELVE

Each time Ash left base camp to invade another village, Rosalie felt new depths of self-loathing for not trying to stop him. She also feared she'd never see him again. Most mornings he stayed in bed with her as long as he could, but he had his duties. Rosalie felt confused at the way she'd grown to depend on him. She wasn't used to it. She hated it and reveled in it all at once.

They'd argued the night before. Ash remained evasive about his plans. Rosalie found it hard to reconcile the gentle man she'd fallen for with the one who left her bed each morning to pull unsuspecting people from their homes.

"I wish you felt like you could confide in me," she'd told him.

"It's best that I don't."

Though spoken gently, his words stung. When she'd tried to press him, he'd shut her down. "You're going to have to trust me," he'd said dismissively.

"You haven't given me a reason to," she'd shot back. It wasn't true. He'd given her many reasons to. But what he was doing couldn't be ignored. She needed a reason for his actions. And she hoped to the gods it was a good one.

Ash climbed out of bed without kissing her good morning and headed to the shower. Rosalie could tell he was angry from their fight. She realized she expected him to be open and honest with her, but she hadn't been completely honest with him. There were things she couldn't reveal to him. But she knew there were things she could. Things she should. She twisted the bedsheets in her hands as she struggled to find the words to begin her confession.

When Ash stepped out of the shower, he wrapped a towel around his waist and crossed the room to the dresser to find a clean change of clothes. He was surprised to find Rosalie sitting up in bed. Her eyes flitted nervously as she stared in his direction.

He pulled clothes from the dresser, shut the drawer, then turned to face her. "What's on your mind?" Setting the clothes at the foot of the bed, he stretched out beside her, towel coming undone.

"I'm no warrior," she blurted out, eyes brimming with tears. She couldn't take the dishonesty any longer.

Smiling broadly, he said, "And you think I wasn't already aware of this?"

A look of confusion swept across her pretty face. "But when I first met you, you said that…"

"Roe, I've been at this game a long time. I can distinguish between the attire of a warrior and that of a huntress."

"Then why did you…"

He sat up, back against the headboard, and shifted her onto his lap. He played with a strand of her auburn hair, wrestling with how much of the truth he should share. "You intrigued me that day. The way you held your ground. The fact the gas didn't work on you and make you bend to my will. I wanted you to believe I had a greater excuse for needing you with me."

She shoved him, playfully. "And I've been so worried that once you found out…"

"I'd what, send you back? Not likely," he chuckled as he leaned in to kiss her.

At first, she returned the kiss, but pushed him away once she recalled more about that day. "But when I refused to cooperate, you were going to house me in a prison cell with those vulgar men." She shuddered at the memory of how helpless she'd felt.

"Oh, c'mon Roe, you know that was never going to happen."

"Well, what would you have done if I hadn't admitted to being a Mender?"

He thought about it, rubbing his chin. "Honestly, I'm not sure. But I promise you, I would have thought of something."

"I was wrong about you," she told him.

"How so?"

"Out of you and Stryker, you're the mean one." But when the hurt look flickered across his face, she laughed. "I'm kidding, Ash. I don't think that."

"Actually, Stryker isn't such a bad guy once you get to know him."

She shrugged, looking doubtful. "Do you have to go today?" she asked, changing the subject.

"Afraid so."

"I suppose Stryker doesn't give you much choice," she said bitterly.

Ash's jaw tightened. There was so much he wanted to explain to her, especially after seeing how torn up she'd been about her mild lie by omission. Instead, he pressed his lips to hers. "I'll be back as soon as the gods allow."

Rosalie's mouth curved in a pout. "You don't even believe in the gods, do you?"

He shook his head *no*.

"And I suppose you think Orthron is the only planet with life on it?"

He paused, pondering for a moment. "No, I suppose there are other planets with fragments of life. But I doubt they hold any intelligent beings like us."

Her eyes twinkled and she flashed him a half-smile.

"Why do I get the feeling you're judging me right now?" he chuckled.

"Oh, I'm judging hard," she teased. "You don't believe in gods. You don't believe in intelligent life on other planets. What do you believe in?"

He leaned in, motioning with his index finger for her to lean in closer. When she tilted her head towards him, he kissed her cheek, then nibbled at her ear. "I believe in the power of persuasion," he whispered.

Heart skipping a beat, she whispered back, "Hmm... I'm starting to believe in that too."

Despite her own powers of persuasion, Rosalie was unable to convince Ash to stay behind. He, Stryker, and the army of men left for another village, leaving her alone with her thoughts. And her guilt.

She thought of seeking out Talon, but didn't know if she could face him. *What sort of person was she to not try and stop these invasions?*

Spending time with Othelia helped brighten her mood. Her friend continued to be of few words but remained a pleasant companion. Sometimes the two hung out in Othelia's room, playing card games while Rosalie rehashed stories from her rebellious teenage years. But most of their free time was spent at the stables. Othelia showed Rosalie how to use a hoof pick and the proper way to inspect and clean the horses' hooves. She also taught her how to braid ribbons into the manes of the magnificent beasts as she patiently explained the significance behind each color of ribbon. Orange, Rosalie learned, was for the horses ridden by the leaders. It represented the color of the sun – which led the way for all mankind by day. Blue, meaning bravery, was for the horses of the seasoned warriors. And red, signifying allegiance, was used for the remaining horses.

Rosalie was tying off the final ribbon, admiring the mare's shiny coat and mane, when she said aloud, "Let's take the horses for a ride."

Othelia's hand froze on the brush she was using to untangle her stallion's mane. She kept her eyes focused on the horse as she said, "I don't think that would be such a good idea."

Rosalie's face fell. For but a moment she'd forgotten where she was – who she was. No matter how deep her feelings grew for Ash, or how accustomed to her circumstances she'd grown, she was no more than his prisoner. The revelation wounded her. She forced a smile. "Of course. What a silly thought. I don't know what I was thinking."

Othelia gave her a sympathetic look, which only made Rosalie feel worse.

Smile plastered on her face, she returned to her grooming regimen. But in her head the warning blared. For the sake of her heart, for the sake of her soul, it was impossible for her to stay.

CHAPTER THIRTEEN

Ash laid awake, watching Rosalie as she slept. She'd been unusually quiet before bed, and now he'd awoken to the sound of her talking in her sleep. Only it wasn't his name on her soft, luscious lips. It was Talon's. She'd murmured it over and over. He hooked an arm around her waist and reveled in the smoothness of her skin as he swallowed the pain of possibly losing her. He knew he shouldn't feel betrayed at the idea of her choosing Talon over him. She'd known the man since childhood. Maybe she'd always loved him. He wondered what he was feeling. Jealousy, perhaps, though he seldom stooped to such a weak emotion. He wanted to punch the wall in disgust. Instead he held her tighter and pressed his lips to her forehead.

Rosalie stirred. When her eyes fluttered open, she sat upright in bed. "I was having a nightmare." She pressed her fingertips to her temples, trying to block out the scenes that still played in her head.

"You were talking in your sleep." He stared over at her, summoning the patience to wait for an explanation.

"Was I? Why didn't you wake me?"

"I wasn't sure if you wanted to be woken up." And there it was, traces of jealousy rising up in him once more. He did his best to squelch it. "What did you dream about?" He kept his tone nonchalant.

"I had a dream there was a great battle. You were riding out in front. And Talon…" Her voice broke. "Talon was killed." Tears slid down her cheeks and she buried her head in Ash's chest.

He put his arms around her and held her tight. He felt relief, followed by guilt. She still had no idea why she was here; why Talon was here. He'd kept her in the dark and counted on her to trust him. It was a big ask.

"Talon is going to be just fine," he finally said.

She wiped her eyes and gazed up at him. "I'd like to see him today."

"What for?"

This time it was her turn to be defensive. "What do you mean *what for*? He's my best friend. You've kept us separated."

Ash drew in a sharp breath. The growing familiarity of jealousy cloaked him like a wet blanket. "Okay," he finally agreed.

"Thank you." She kissed his cheek and laid her head on his chest.

"Not so fast," he said. "I have one condition."

She sat back up in bed and peered over at him. "What's that?"

His eyes narrowed. "You tell me Talon's power."

Rosalie looked stunned. Then torn. "He has no power," she lied.

She knew the moment the lie passed her lips that Ash didn't believe her. His eyes grew dark and disappointment clouded his face. "Wh-what I should have said," she stammered, "was what makes you think he has a power?"

- 84 -

"The gas," Ash said flatly.

"What?"

He exhaled, searching for the right amount of information to divulge. "The gas we used on your village. It didn't work on him. Or you. That's how we usually know. It's specifically formulated not to work on *variants*."

Rosalie crossed her arms and tried not to be offended. "Why wouldn't you want to subdue *variants*? Wouldn't they... wouldn't *we* potentially be the most dangerous?"

He remained silent. He knew he'd already revealed too much. He needed to protect his men. He also needed to protect her, and sometimes that meant protecting her from the truth.

"We have our reasons," he defended.

"You want to enslave us to be part of your army I suppose? It won't work. Talon will never fight alongside you." She didn't argue that she wouldn't. She could no longer be sure.

"There's more to us than that," he said angrily.

"Then enlighten me." Her green eyes flashed with rage. She crossed her arms, challenging him to reveal his plans.

He climbed out of bed to avoid her, dressing quickly. "I'll arrange for you to see your friend," he finally said. A knock at the door interrupted their quarrel. "That's Stryker," he spoke sharply. "I've got to go. I'll see you later." He bent down and kissed her forehead, then stalked out of the room without another word.

When Rosalie stepped out of her room, she was surprised to find a guard waiting to escort her to meet up with Talon. It pleased her that, despite being cross with her, Ash was true to his word. The guard led her to the outer courtyard, where Talon was already waiting. "I'll be right over here," the guard said, stepping out of earshot but keeping the pair in his line of sight.

Still reeling from her nightmare, Rosalie felt a flood of relief at seeing her old friend looking well. She hadn't seen him since they'd first arrived at the inn. It had only been a few weeks, but it felt like ages. Talon's hair and beard were grown out more than usual, his loose-fitting clothing suggested he may have lost some weight, but he remained vibrant and his coloring was good.

"It's so great to see you, Roe," he said, lifting her up and swinging her around before setting her back down. "Everything still … okay?" His eyes searched hers.

Her face turned crimson, but she shook her head, *yes.* "They're keeping me around to use my mending powers is all," she said nonchalantly, only revealing partial truths. It was the first time she'd lied to her friend.

"That's good. That's good." He smoothed her hair, then let his hands rest on her shoulders. "I've been so worried about you."

She gazed up at him. "We're not kids anymore. You don't have to protect me. Not like before." She shivered as her darkest memory from sixteen played in her head. The scar on her shoulder blade seemed to burn. She reached behind and skimmed her fingertips over it.

He frowned and gave her shoulders a gentle squeeze. "I wish I could have gotten there sooner."

"Talon, we've been over this. It's not your fault. And you got there in plenty of time. Things could have been much worse." She shivered again, and he pulled her into his embrace.

"One of the men asked what your power was," she said, pulling back from him and switching the subject. She didn't dare speak Ash's name in front of Talon. She feared speaking his name aloud to her childhood friend would reveal her feelings.

"How do they know I have a power?"

"That's what I asked. I guess the gas they used at our village is purposely designed not to work on those with mutated genes."

"Is it meant to weed us out, then?"

"That's my assumption, but that's all the information I have."

Talon stroked his growing beard. "Tell them."

"Tell them what? About your power?"

He nodded. "I don't mind. What do I have to lose? Maybe they'll find me useful and it'll guarantee they'll keep me alive."

"I don't think they plan to kill us."

"But we don't know that, Roe. That's why we have to play it smart. We have to plan our escape."

"That's why I'm here," she explained. "They're moving in on another village in a couple of hours. It's always chaos when they leave and return. We need to study it – plan the best path of escape based on it. They seem to raid a new village at least every couple of days. We need to use the chaos of one of those raids as our window of opportunity."

Talon took her hand in his and the two put their heads together to form an escape plan. But as they plotted, she couldn't help but wonder what she'd be escaping to.

It was late afternoon when she returned to the room she shared with Ash. He wasn't there yet, not that she expected him to be. It was too early. She started a bath and lit a candle. The steam from the bathtub fogged up the bathroom mirror. She leaned forward to un-fog it and studied her reflection. A conflicted soul stared back at her. Escaping with her friend and rejoining her village should be the right thing to do. So why did she feel so guilty?

She stripped off her clothes and lowered herself into the tub. The scalding water stung her skin. She closed her eyes and immersed herself, dunking her head below the steaming water. She held her breath and counted backwards from ten. When she rose to the surface, Ash stood above her, staring into the tub.

"What are you doing?" he asked.

The heat on Rosalie's skin wasn't just from the bath. "Contemplating," she admitted.

Ash cocked his head to the side and shot her a questioning look. "About?"

"He's a Blocker," she blurted out.

"Pardon?"

"Talon. His power is that he's a Blocker. He's able to block the powers of others. It's a blessing and a curse. While he can't fall prey to a Seducer, and is immune to an Inflictor, he can't benefit from the powers of a Healer or a Mender. You know, a Blocker."

"I haven't heard much about Blockers." Ash didn't hide his disappointment.

"His powers can be extended beyond himself," she interjected, fearing if Ash and his army didn't find Talon useful, they may get rid of him.

"How so?"

"If he is in physical contact with someone, and concentrates hard enough, he can act as a Blocker for that person too."

A smiled played across his lips. "That could be useful."

"I'm glad my friend can finally be of use to you," she muttered, unable to mask the bitterness in her tone.

"I'm sorry, I didn't mean it the way it sounded."

She started to rise from the bath, but Ash placed a hand on her shoulder, gently pressing her back down. "I was thinking I might join you."

She wanted to tell him he wasn't invited, but her heart slammed in her chest and her body ached to be closer to him. *Yes*, she decided definitively as she watched with lust and hunger while he stripped off his clothes; she was indeed a conflicted soul.

CHAPTER FOURTEEN

When Stryker barged into the bedroom in the early light of day, Ash felt Rosalie stiffen beside him. He reached for her hand beneath the covers and gave it a reassuring squeeze. "To what do I owe this interruption," Ash said, voice dripping with sarcasm.

"Time to go," Stryker barked. His hair was pulled back, revealing his full scar. His lip curled and he didn't bother to hide his disdain at seeing Rosalie in Ash's bed.

Ash nodded in acceptance and Stryker stalked out of the room without another word. Rosalie exhaled slowly and her body relaxed.

He pulled her closer, needing to assure her. "He won't hurt you, Roe."

She turned on her side to face him. "What makes you so sure?"

He smoothed her hair. "Because I told him not to."

She propped her elbow on the pillow and rested her cheek on her open palm. "And you're so sure your fearless leader will listen to you?" She kept her demeanor flippant as she struggled to keep her emotions in check.

He paused, channeling his patience. He wanted to correct her statement but couldn't reveal the truth yet. "You're just going to have to trust me," he said, taking her silky, auburn hair between his fingertips and tucking a strand behind her ear.

"Trust the one who drugged my village, kidnapped me, and is keeping me as some sort of sex slave?" Her cheeks burned, and tears of anger crept in her eyes.

The words stung. Ash knew in his gut he'd never forced her; but now he second-guessed himself. "Is that what's happening here?" Keeping his tone soft, but firm, he searched her eyes for the truth.

"No," she admitted after a bit, looking down in misery. She knew her hurtful words were coming from a place of insecurity, and she hated herself for it.

Ash tipped her chin upward, forcing her to look at him. "This thing happening between us. You and me. You are free to be out of it at any time."

Rosalie's face grew hot. She'd been trying so hard to convince herself it was all an act; it was hard for her to admit her true feelings. Her throat constricted. "I want to stay," she whispered.

"I'm sorry, what was that?" he prodded, cupping his ear with his hand and leaning in closer.

"You heard me," she said forcefully, shoving him in frustration. She struggled to keep her tears at bay.

He chuckled and pulled her into his arms, kissing the top of her head. "I want you to stay too, Roe," he admitted. "Dammit, if you're not going to be the death of me though."

She laid her head on his chest and let him stroke her hair. Confusion and doubt surrounded her, but through all these emotions, she felt his strength. She felt love – which made what she planned to do seem impossible.

"I didn't realize you'd designated yourself as my alarm clock," Ash told Stryker once he'd joined him in the stables.

"We have a schedule to keep."

"Have you ever known me to be late?"

"No. But I've also never known you to..." He paused, words trailing off.

"To what?"

"To be so bloody irresponsible," he spat out.

"You need to mind your own business."

"When it comes to the affairs of these men," he gestured towards the group of men busy mounting up for the day, "it is my business."

"Do you honestly think I'd jeopardize the safety of these men? For what? Some skirt?"

Stryker remained silent.

"You do, don't you? Well, Stryker, if that's what you think, you really don't know me at all."

Pulling himself up on the horse, Stryker took the reins, then looked down at Ash. "Right now, I think I know you more than you know yourself."

Ash's jaw tightened. He wanted to argue but knew there was a ring of truth to what Stryker said. He hadn't come to terms with his feelings for Rosalie. He'd started to rely on her. After every raid, it was her he longed to rush back to. What was he to do with the beautiful woman who came to his bed each night, offering herself so freely without expecting anything in return? Not even her freedom.

CHAPTER FIFTEEN

Rosalie slipped out of her room and crept towards the horse stalls to meet Talon. The pair were counting on the chaos of the army returning from the latest raid. With the flurry of horses and new prisoners, they hoped to go unnoticed.

The plan was to steal two horses and make a clean break towards the cover of the forest. Rosalie had secured blankets and enough food for two days' ride, which she'd stashed behind one of the troughs. What she hadn't managed to do was shake the stabbing agony of regret at leaving Ash behind without saying goodbye. She shrugged off the unwelcome emotion, telling herself she didn't owe him an explanation – or anything else.

Talon wasn't at the stables when she arrived. For a moment she fantasized he'd changed his mind, giving her an excuse to stay with Ash. But she dismissed the foolish thought and rounded the stalls to look for him. She found him at the edge of the courtyard, standing awkwardly in the open. He had a peculiar look on his face, and Rosalie immediately knew something wasn't right. When she rushed over to him, Stryker and a host of his men rode up beside her.

Stryker dismounted, then crossed his arms in front of his chest, glowering at her. "I'm impressed. She did just as you said she would." He looked at Talon and grinned.

Rosalie stood in stunned silence as she watched Talon cross the courtyard and stand beside Stryker.

"You betrayed me," she choked out as the revelation sunk in. Tears of anger stung her green eyes.

"I'm sorry, Roe, I didn't have a choice." He dipped his head, ashamed.

"You always have a choice," she hissed.

His head whipped upward, and his eyes narrowed. "Yeah, well some of us don't have the luxury of sleeping with our captor to guarantee our safety," he spat back.

His words were a blow, and tears of shame and humiliation slid down her cheeks.

"What's going on here?" Ash spoke up from behind her, startling everyone. He was on foot and no one heard him approach.

She turned in anger to face him. In doing so, she noticed a cut above his right eye, but resisted the urge to ask him about it. It was her own skin she needed to worry about. "I guess this was your big plan all along?" she accused. "What in the name of Helstice were you stringing me along for?"

"Roe, I don't know what you're talking about." He sounded more confused than defensive.

"Oh, save it. I can only take so much lies and betrayal in one day."

He placed his hands on her shoulders and held her gaze. "Roe, seriously…"

"Someone needs to teach this girl a lesson," Stryker said, stepping towards Rosalie.

Ash looked sharply at Stryker, then held up his right hand. When Stryker advanced, Ash made a circular motion with his index finger, chanting something under his breath as a faint glow of light resonated from his fingertips.

Stryker stopped in his tracks. His countenance changed and he bowed his head in obedience, appearing to shrink in stature.

At first Rosalie was confused, but then the realization hit her. "You're a Seducer," she said, turning to Ash in disbelief. Her eyes pleaded for him to deny it. Instead, he nodded, and Rosalie's knees nearly buckled. The shocking truth took the breath out of her lungs and the wind out of her sails.

She'd met a Seducer once. He'd passed through her village, charming people into giving up their livestock, jewelry, and other valuables before he waltzed out of town. The impact had been devastating. Rosalie recognized the power, and all at once it became clear.

She couldn't keep the tears from falling. Her shoulders shook in anger as feelings of frustration, betrayal, and self-loathing washed over her all at once. He hadn't cared about her. And truly, she hadn't cared about him. He had held her under his spell so he could use her until he was done with her.

Erupting in anger, she shoved Ash as hard as she could, then broke into a run, headed for the line of trees in the distance.

"Grab her," Stryker barked to one of the men, snapping out of the spell.

"Let her go," Ash said. When Stryker started to argue, Ash shot him a warning look. "We don't need her anymore," he said sharply. But his eyes clouded with regret.

Tears blurred Rosalie's vision as she ran as fast as her legs would allow. She was sobbing hysterically, and her heart beat wildly in her chest at the thought of what might happen if she were caught. Would Stryker order his men to shoot her in the back while she fled? Then she realized – they were Ash's men, not Stryker's. She'd been played.

As she ran, she tried to imagine how the man who'd held her in his arms and kissed her so tenderly could be so deceitful. Would he be so cruel as to give the order himself? To counter the possible threat, she ran in a zigzag line towards the trees. To her surprise, she didn't hear gunshots. Not even shouts from her captors. She heard only the thud of her footfalls and the bitter cries that escaped her lips.

When she reached the cover of the woods, she paused to take a breath behind a mammoth fir tree. She bent forward, placing her hands on her knees. She closed her eyes and concentrated on returning her breathing pattern to normal. She wiped her eyes with her shirtsleeve and drew in a long, sharp breath before standing upright once more.

Feeling some assurance from being tucked behind the massive tree, Rosalie peered around its edges to view her captors. They remained a far distance away. She could make out Stryker and Ash in what appeared to be a heated argument, but nobody pursued her.

She hadn't had time to consider how she'd feel once she escaped. Relief, at a minimum. A sense of pride. Perhaps a bit terrified at the prospect of being caught. But hidden behind the tree and panting from her exhilarating run, she felt none of those things. Instead she felt something unexpected. Regret. Regret and loneliness. *Who was she without Ash, and just what was she supposed to do now?*

Ash wanted to go after Rosalie, but he knew it would make him look weak. No Seducer's spell would help him overcome showing weakness to his men. He also knew she needed a cooling off period. One night alone in the woods ought to do it. The temperatures wouldn't dip low enough this time of year to put her in any real danger. He knew it would be cold enough to make her reconsider running again, though. He worried what she would do if she came face-to-face with a wild animal, but he'd also witnessed her in action and knew she could protect herself. He thought about the short-blade knife she kept hidden in a sheath tied to her inner thigh. No, he decided. She would be safe. Hungry. Cold. But safe.

At first light, Ash slipped past his men and into the woods to find the woman who'd slain his heart. He'd had a sleepless night as he'd reevaluated his original decision not to tell Rosalie he was in charge. He'd been so convinced it was the right thing to do. Now part of him wondered if he'd done it so he wouldn't have to carry the full weight of his guilt for invading her village; or suffer through her glaring at him with the same disdain as she did Stryker. He'd pondered all these things as he tossed and turned in the overwhelmingly empty bed. But as restless as his night had been, he knew hers had been worse. He'd at least had a bed. And heat. He figured their regrets were about equal.

He found her a few rows deep into the tree line, nestled under a blanket of leaves and twigs. He shook his head. He knew they wouldn't have afforded much warmth. In a small way, it pleased him to discover she hadn't gone far. It gave him hope.

"Roe," he whispered, but she didn't answer, feigning sleep. He picked her up with minimal effort. He knew she was awake, but he let her save face and didn't call her out on it. Her body was cold as ice, and he pressed her close as he carried her back to his room. She buried her face in his chest, soaking up his warmth.

He brought her into his room and laid her on the bed. Rosalie shivered, chilled to the bone. She looked up at him, wary and a little afraid.

"I'll draw you a bath," he said tersely.

Rosalie tried to remove her damp clothing, but her fingers were too stiff to comply. She fumbled with the buttons of her blouse.

"Let me do it," Ash spoke from the doorway of the bathroom.

Ignoring him, she continued to struggle with the buttons.

"I'll do it," he said gruffly, moving towards her and pushing her hands away. He worked quickly to unbutton her blouse.

Cheeks burning and heart pounding, Rosalie refused to look at him. He pulled her up from the bed and jerked her wet shirt from her body. He made quick work of removing the rest of her clothing as she stood there, helpless and shivering. His movements were calculated and efficient. Then, without warning, he swooped her into his arms. She felt his strong hands as he carried her, naked, towards the bathroom and she made no effort of retreat.

When he lowered her into the tub, the piping hot water stung her skin, but she welcomed its gentle assault. The night had been rough, and she thought she'd never be warm again. She leaned her head back. The tops of her breasts hovered above the water's surface – pert, inviting. After stripping off his clothes, Ash climbed into the tub behind her, cradling her in his arms as he kissed her neck.

Rosalie felt warmth and desire stir her blood. "Don't," she pleaded.

"Don't what?"

She twisted her body to face him. She tried to establish some distance between them, but her knees brushed his. "Please don't use your charms on me. It's not playing fair." Tears escaped her eyes and slid down her cheeks.

Ash cupped her chin in his hand, forcing her to look at him. "I would never do that to you."

She shrugged her shoulders. She didn't believe him. Or perhaps she didn't want to believe him. If he had charmed her, she wouldn't need to hold herself responsible for the deep feelings she harbored for this man who was her enemy.

"Roe, I would never hurt you. I would never let anyone else hurt you. And I would never, ever use a spell or a charm on you without your knowledge. I played fair."

Her tears flowed easily now. She didn't try to stop them. "I don't believe you," she choked out.

"Yes, you do, Love. That's why you're so upset. You don't want to admit you might have real feelings for someone like me." He didn't sound angry. A little hurt. But mostly matter-of-fact.

"And what about you?" she asked, trying to sound tough.

"What about me?"

"Do you... What are your feelings?" Her face burned as she launched the question into the universe and allowed herself to be vulnerable.

Ash appeared taken back; stunned into silence.

"I guess I figured as much," she said, interpreting his silence as rejection.

"I'm crazy about you, Roe," he blurted out. He cleared his throat, uncomfortable with expressing his feelings so openly. But he would do so if it meant that much to her; if it meant he would no longer have to see her cry.

She sniffed and looked away, trying to process the emotions his words stirred in her. He didn't say he loved her, but it was a start.

"Roe," he spoke softly.

"Stop," she said, shaking with emotion.

"Roe, this is real. You and me. I freaking love you if you want to know the truth." He gathered her in his arms, and she rested her cheek against his bare chest. "Roe, when I thought you might be gone for good, I didn't know what to do. I love you, and that's something you're going to have to get used to."

She smiled up at him. Her red-rimmed eyes were swollen, but they held a warm glow. "And you swear you didn't use any spells on me?" she asked, but this time her question was playful. She knew the answer.

"I swear to the goddess, Anteria."

"You don't even believe in Anteria."

"But I know you do. And I swear by that. Is it so hard to believe you could have real feelings for someone like me?" He smiled, but he looked pained. He was all nerves as he waited for her response.

"I don't want to hurt anymore," she whispered, eyes cast down in misery.

He pulled her close and brushed the hair out of her green eyes. "Then don't, Roe. Let it go. Take a chance with me."

She gulped back her tears. "You put me in danger of being hurt more than anyone or anything else."

"And what about me? You don't think you do the same? Half my men out there think I've gone crazy, soft – or both. But I don't care. I'm ready to take that leap with you."

She crossed her arms in front of her chest, her stubborn side taking the wheel.

"You need to decide if you're ready to do the same," he finished.

"I *want* to be," she spoke softly.

He felt gutted. "I'm afraid that's not good enough."

Tears rolled down her cheeks. "I just want to be sure what I feel is real."

"And what do you think you feel?"

She hesitated, letting him suffer for a moment. Finally, she admitted, "I love you too, Ash."

"Thank the gods." Breathing a heavy sigh of relief, he leaned in and kissed her. His mouth felt warm on hers and she pressed closer to him, lengthening the kiss. The water was waxing cold, so he stood and scooped her out of the tub. She squealed with delight as he brought her to the bed and plopped her down unceremoniously.

"You're such a brute," she teased.

"Hey, you told me not to use my charms."

"I meant not to use your powers. I don't think it would hurt to use the natural charms you were born with."

"Nah, they're overrated." His eyes gleamed as he grinned back at her. He pulled back the covers and they both climbed in.

Rosalie was still shivering, but mostly with anticipation. She knew this time when Ash made love to her, she'd have no doubts it was real. His words. Her feelings. She was elated.

"I can just hold you if you want," he told her, but the desire in his tone begged for much more.

"I want to feel all of you."

"I can't say no to that." He pulled her towards him. For the first time, they came together as lovers on an even playing field.

"I see that Rosalie's back," Stryker said to Ash over breakfast, arching an eyebrow. "Thought you decided we didn't need her."

His jaw tightened and he shrugged in response.

"I wouldn't have hurt her, you know. I was just trying to scare her."

Ash nodded but his eyes burned with anger. He didn't say anything, unsure of what might come out. The altercation still infuriated him, but he didn't want to throw away a long friendship by saying something he'd regret.

"Ash, I get that she's pretty and all, but..."

"I think I love her," he blurted out, glancing over at his friend, then back at the ground. But it was a mild lie. He already knew he loved her.

Stryker nodded, lost in thought, but somehow not surprised. He'd never seen his friend fall so hard. There was a time he would have seen it as a weakness; but he remembered his own plunge into love. Subconsciously he patted his shirt pocket where he kept the picture of his wife and baby tucked beneath his stash of bitterroot. "I hear you. Now what are you going to do about it?"

Ash rubbed his temples, deep in thought. He skimmed his fingers over the cut above his eye – a much-too-recent reminder of how the last raid had almost gone awry. *Was he losing control?* "I don't know," he finally said.

Stryker stood to his feet, brushing imaginary dirt from his pants. "You'd better figure it out."

CHAPTER SIXTEEN

"**S**teady," Ash whispered, his lips inches from Rosalie's ear. He pretended not to notice the intoxicating way she smelled, or the way his loins tightened in response to being so close to her.

"I *have* done this before," she whispered back, pretending to be annoyed by his hovering. She'd missed the thrill of the hunt; how it felt when the grip of the bow rested on the pad of her thumb. She adjusted her stance and softened her hold. She knew in the excitement she was squeezing the grip too tightly.

The tuskentee crouched in the brush but was too massive to go unnoticed. Head like a deer, but with a body resembling a brown bear, the tuskentee had an abundance of meat and would sustain the soldiers for some time. All eyes were on Rosalie as she prepared to bring the beast down.

When Ash had announced earlier that morning that his army would not travel to any of the villages, but instead take the day to rest up, Rosalie was pleased. But she was ecstatic when she learned he was going to take a small group on a hunt. She expected him to argue when she offered to go along. Instead he obliged her.

The hunting party had been tracking the impressive beast for hours. Now a half-dozen arrows were trained on the animal, but Rosalie had the best position. She licked her lips, pulled the bowstring back, then released it and let the arrow fly.

The arrow's tip struck the animal in the heart, dropping it. Without hesitation, she plucked her spear from the ground and ran towards the magnificent beast. Ash surged forward, a long-blade knife in hand. To Rosalie's relief, the animal was already dead. She felt comforted it hadn't suffered. She knelt beside it, stroking its soft fur and murmuring a short chant.

"For pity's sake, don't try and mend the beast," Ash teased.

Rosalie grinned up at him. "It was a prayer of thanks to Baskkton, god of the hunt," she explained, rising to her feet. She wiped the dirt from her knees and shot him a playful look that seemed to say: *didn't your parents teach you anything?*

Ash grinned back at her. He'd never been a believer in the gods, but he admired Rosalie's unwavering faith and dedication. It made her seem all the more innocent.

"Whoever killed it gets to carry it out," Othelia teased, coming up behind Ash.

"Does that also mean I get to choose who eats it?" Rosalie challenged.

"Fine, we'll help you," Othelia said, laughing. She embraced her friend, then knelt beside the fallen beast. "Clean kill," she praised. "Baskkton will be appeased."

Ash rolled his eyes. "Oh no, not you too."

"Not a believer?" Othelia mused.

"Hopelessly incredulous," Rosalie laughed.

When the hunting party returned to base camp, a roaring campfire had already been prepared. By the bursts of laughter from the men, it was obvious a break from the raids was what they needed.

"Thank you for convincing Ash to take me," Rosalie told Othelia.

Her friend grew embarrassed. "Who says I had anything to do with it?"

Rosalie placed her hands on her hips and cocked her head to the side.

"Fine," Othelia said, smiling. "You are welcome. It was great seeing you in action."

"I'd forgotten how much I've missed that."

"You know what you probably don't miss?"

"What's that?"

Othelia jerked her thumb in the direction of the fallen tuskentee. "Skinning and cleaning the kill."

Groaning, she said, "I vote we give that lovely task to one of the men." She batted her eyes and placed her hand on her heart. "I'm but a frail female, I think I need to take a warm bath."

Othelia laughed. "I like how you think. Go have your bath and meet me at the stables in an hour. I've also convinced Ash to let us take the horses out for a run."

"Thank you for today," Rosalie told Ash later that evening.

Never one to be good at receiving praise, he grunted in response.

"You know, while I was riding bareback through the woods, I had a thought," she said, looking hesitant. "What if we tried something tonight?"

"What did you have in mind?" He raised an eyebrow.

The heat of his gaze pierced her soul and surged through her body. "I want to use my powers on you." She bit her lip and gazed shyly at him.

"Darlin', I'm pretty sure you already have." He grinned and pulled her close.

Gently pushing him away, she said, "No, I mean…"

"I know what you mean," he told her, holding her gaze with intensity. "But it's only fair if I can do the same."

She pondered for a moment. It wasn't easy for her to give up control. But then again, it was no easier for Ash – and wasn't she asking the same of him?

"Okay," she finally agreed.

"Okay then. Do we need a safe word?" he teased. He cupped her buttocks in his hands and playfully nipped at her earlobe.

"I think we can handle ourselves."

Rosalie's heart beat wildly as Ash moved in closer. As he framed her face with his hands, he asked, "Do you trust me?"

She nodded. "I trust you implicitly."

"Hmm, doubtful," he said, flashing her a grin.

"I *mostly* trust you implicitly," she amended. Her green eyes glowed with amusement. And desire.

A deep, throaty laugh escaped his lips. He kissed her softly, then closed his eyes in concentration as his hands caressed her face. Rosalie could feel something stir within her. It was more than desire. It was as if she and Ash were the only two people on Orthron and the universe orbited around them. Her body hummed, and a deep warmth spread through her unlike anything she'd felt before. When he leaned down to kiss her, she stood on her tiptoes to meet his mouth as it claimed hers.

Dizzy with excitement, she closed her eyes and trailed her fingers down Ash's back. He tensed, then relaxed as she let her soothing charm begin. She could feel his tension alleviate through her fingertips. His shoulders drew slack, but his breathing became erratic as his desire built.

When he began to undress her, she felt completely at ease. She didn't worry about the ugly scar on her shoulder blade, or the smallness of her breasts. Her insecurities melted away because she knew all she was, it was enough for him.

She touched the cut above Ash's eye and murmured the mending chant her mother taught her. She pulled his head towards her lips and kissed the wound with her Mender's lips.

Ash grinned at her, then lifted her towards him. She wrapped her arms around his neck and her legs around his hips. He slid her downward until he fit inside her. She felt his fullness and her head lulled back as she sighed with desire. He pressed her against the wall as he moved his hips, pushing deeper with each thrust.

Rosalie's skin felt slick against his and Ash fought to keep his control. He murmured something in her ear; an ancient charm, she suspected. His words cut straight to her heart and she was overpowered by her feelings for him.

Her heart swelled until she thought it might burst. Emotions running high, she feared she might suffocate beneath the weight of them. Her vision blurred as her other senses heightened. She was losing control. "No more," she begged.

Startled, Ash slid out of her and set her down gently, steadying her when her legs wobbled. "You okay, Roe?" he asked. "Did I hurt you?"

"No," she reassured him, looking embarrassed. "I didn't mean for you to stop. I just … What I felt was…" She looked down at the floor, unsure how to explain herself.

He took her by the hand and led her back to the bed. He sat down next to her and slung an arm over her tiny shoulders.

"That was just more than I expected." Her heart still beat wildly.

"Me too," he whispered. He planted a soft kiss on her bare shoulder.

"Maybe no magic this time?" she suggested, looking up at him.

He smiled at her, tugging playfully at her hair. "Who says what you were feeling was magic?"

He pushed her down on the bed and stretched his body over hers. She gazed up at him, longingly. "I need you Ash." She didn't just need him to make love to her. She needed him in ways she'd never needed anyone. Or wanted to need anyone. It left her raw, vulnerable, and completely out of her element.

"I need you too, Roe," he told her. And he meant it in every way she did. He kissed her stomach, then her inner thigh as she squirmed with anticipation.

When he made love to her, it was slow and gentle. He needed her to know she was loved; that what she was feeling was real. He wanted to feel her body against his, hear her beg for her release, and to know without a doubt she loved him in return. It was important to him they both knew they were together for the right reasons. He was no more her captor than she was his. "Give it to me," he told her, when he sensed she was getting close.

"No, Ash, I want more," she begged.

He deepened his thrusts. The pair moved together, the intensity building. "Is this enough for you?" he growled seductively.

In response, Rosalie arched her hips and screamed out as she climaxed. Her release was Ash's undoing. He called out her name as he lost himself inside her.

CHAPTER SEVENTEEN

"Spit it out," Rosalie said, setting down her bowl of mush on the tree stump she shared with Ash. He had joined her for breakfast, but his brooding silence was keeping her off-balance. "You clearly have something you want to say, so just say it." Her no-nonsense tone told him her patience was wearing thin.

"Come with me today," he said, reaching for her hand.

She snatched her hand away and folded her arms in front of her chest in defiance. "To invade someone's home? I want no part of it."

Ash paused, his pride and patience being tested. "You don't have to do much. I want you to see we're not the monsters you've made us out to be in your head."

She glared at him. She didn't see a monster staring back at her. She saw a man she cared deeply for. A man who was passionate about his cause – whatever that cause might be. But she couldn't overlook the fact that it came at the expense of others.

"I'll pass."

"Roe, you know I wouldn't ask you if it wasn't important." He couldn't mask his regret. When she didn't respond, he continued. "The city doesn't have walls surrounding it. The villagers will see my men from a long way off and may ride out to try and stop us. If we're unable to incapacitate everyone at once, risk of injuries, even casualties, is much higher."

She frowned and her brow furrowed in thought. On the one hand, she didn't approve of the raids and didn't want any part of them. On the other, she couldn't live with herself if she had the chance to prevent casualties and didn't act on it. She took a labored breath. "What do you need from me?"

"The village was recently hit with a bout of sickness. You can ride ahead and offer your mending services. Convince everyone to gather at a central location. That'll provide enough of a distraction for us to sneak in and use the gas more effectively."

Rosalie remained silent, soaking in the magnitude of his request. She was angry with him for asking her when he knew how strongly she felt against the raids. Even more angry with herself for entertaining his request. "Fine," she finally mumbled.

"Thank you, Roe, you won't regret it."

"I already do." With bitter tears welling up, she stood up and stalked away.

Sensing she needed time alone to process everything, Ash didn't go after her. Asking her to do him this favor didn't sit well. But Marx had convinced him it was the only way. All he could think was that his old friend better not have gotten this wrong. It very well may have changed the way Rosalie felt about him forever. War was about sacrifice – but the thought of losing her seemed like a sacrifice too heavy to bear.

When the soldiers neared the village of Amanatria on horseback, Rosalie's arms tightened around Ash's waist. Despite her anger, she kissed the back of his neck. He lifted one hand off the reins and covered her hand with his. His hand felt firm and warm against hers.

They dismounted about a half-mile from the city. As Rosalie prepared to walk the remainder of the way to the village, Ash took her by the hand. "Maybe we should rethink this."

She pulled her hand away. "You got me into this. Your men are all waiting. I'd say it's a bit late for that."

"Then you're on board with this?"

"I'll never be fully onboard with this," she corrected. "I'm doing this to prevent casualties. Not for you."

Ash's jaw tightened, but he nodded in understanding.

"Now I'll need about an hour," she said.

"An hour?" Stryker interrupted.

She shot him a warning look. She wasn't about to let him intimidate her. "You're using my mending powers as a ruse to gather everyone together. I plan to actually use those mending powers for good before you guys come storming in with your gas and bullish ways. Now does anyone have a problem with that?"

Before anyone could argue, she turned on her heel and headed toward Amanatria.

When she arrived at the village, she wasn't met with any probing stares. In fact, the streets were mostly empty. Those bustling about outdoors appeared unphased by her presence.

"Does your village have a PA system?" she asked a woman passing by. The woman responded with a blank stare.

"A public address system," Rosalie explained. "Something to communicate announcements in case of emergencies?"

"Sure," the woman said. "Our town chieftain likes to use it to make *important* announcements." She rolled her eyes. "It's that way," she said, pointing frontward. "Towards the marketplace."

Rosalie thanked her, then hurried in the direction the woman pointed. When she arrived at the marketplace, she was surprised by the lack of people. Despite the dozens of booths of assorted fruit and furs, few came to make a trade.

"Where is everybody?" she asked an elderly man selling brightly colored scarves.

"People have been getting sick," he explained. "Most are too afraid to come outdoors."

"I see." Rosalie smiled warmly but felt plagued with guilt. "Thank you for your time." Glancing around, she saw an outbuilding marked *Chieftain's Office* and made her way towards it.

"Are you the chieftain?" she asked the portly man sitting behind a desk littered with paperwork and empty food wrappers.

"I am," the man said proudly. He circled around the desk and stretched out his hand towards hers. When she took it, he pumped it vigorously. "Chieftain Brotsun, at your service. How may I help you?"

When she explained she'd heard his village had been plagued by illness and that she was a Mender, Brotsun was happy to oblige her request to gather the townspeople together so she could use her mending powers. He insisted, however, on making the announcement himself; a request that Rosalie was happy to oblige.

With a promise of hope for their ailing loved ones, it didn't take long for the villagers to flood the marketplace. Rosalie wrestled with her emotions as she calmly directed the crowd into an organized line.

Sweating from exertion, but eyes gleaming with satisfaction that her mending powers were having an immediate effect on the illness, Rosalie patted the hand of her final patient. But her feelings were replaced by guilt and sorrow once the canisters were launched into the marketplace – into the very spot she'd convinced the naive townspeople to gather. Bitter tears stung her eyes. How had she become this person who stood by while this helpless village was plundered? To her relief, there were no screams from the villagers, no dramatic pleas for help. She witnessed only murmurs of confusion, followed by silence.

Ash waited the appropriate amount of time, then gave the signal for his men to enter the city.

Rosalie recognized the posture of the townspeople. A wave of nostalgia and nausea engulfed her at once as she observed the swaying bodies and vacant stares of those around her. She felt dizzy and her vision blurred. Fearful she might topple over, she took a seat on a nearby bench. From there she had a front row seat to the invasion. She leaned back, arms crossed, and prepared to judge harshly.

As Ash wielded his powers, Rosalie watched in amazement. He spoke in hushed tones to the immobilized villagers. When met with opposition, he chanted softly – assuredly. "You will awake feeling at peace. All will be well," she heard him say. She shook her head to clear it, doing her best to avoid his hypnotic presence. But watching him work, she finally saw him clearly for the first time. He genuinely cared about these people. He did what he needed to keep them safe.

Two *variants* were found amongst the villagers. Both were men – one old, one young. Rosalie didn't know what their powers were, but recognized their scared, puzzled faces and the way their alertness set them apart from the rest. As the *variants* were being led to a wagon, she hurried to join them.

"I myself was taken from Mabel Village. These people mean you no harm," she told the two men. "Everything will be revealed in good time." The men glared back at her with accusing stares, but she hoped her words brought comfort. She could have used them not so long ago.

When it was time to leave, Ash wore a smug grin as he helped Rosalie onto the horse. As they rode away, she cast a final glance back at the swaying villagers. They looked peaceful; like they were sleeping standing up.

"Well?" Ash asked once they'd returned to base camp and were behind closed doors.

"Well, what?"

"Is that what you imagined?"

She frowned, considering. "You're still stealing and taking people against their will."

He looked disappointed. "Is everything black and white with you?"

"That did put my mind at ease quite a bit," she admitted.

"Why do I feel like there's a 'but' coming?"

She offered a tight smile. "*But* I wish you'd find an alternative."

He nodded and pulled her close, kissing her on the top of the head. "I wish that too," he whispered.

Instead of being comforted by his words, she pulled back in anger. "Not good enough," she told him.

"What's that supposed to mean?"

"It means I want to know exactly what's going on. I'm sick of being in the dark. I'm tired of following you like a mindless dolt."

"You really want to know?" he challenged. His tone held a warning that she might get more than she bargained for.

"I think I've *earned* the right to know."

"Your people are at odds with Castle Druin, so I assume you've heard of their leader, Zebadiah."

"Lord Zebadiah?"

"A lord by his own making," Ash said, eyes burning with anger. "He keeps a Receptor in his employ – a woman by the name of Siranya. She can weed out anyone with a special power simply by being in the same room with them. Zebadiah wants full control and is threatened by anyone who might be more powerful than him. He's attacking smaller cities, reviving the purity crusades; only he's collecting *variants* instead of killing them."

"But what about the Coopetition Treaty?"

"That bogus peace treaty between the townships? Lord Zebadiah only signed that thing to buy himself more time. While everyone is busy patting themselves on the back for finally negotiating peace, Lord Zebadiah is building his arsenal. And his army."

"But why hasn't anyone tried to stop him? There hasn't been any news of these attacks."

"He doesn't leave any witnesses." Ash paused, allowing Rosalie to feel the weight of his words, then continued. "He invades villages, wipes out everyone without a power, and takes the *variants* as his prisoners. He justifies his kills by claiming it's punishment for housing society's *unpure*."

The color drained from Rosalie's face. "How do you know this isn't just a terrible rumor? Who could be capable of something so horrible?"

"I've seen first-hand what Lord Zebadiah is capable of." He drew in a sharp breath, then exhaled slowly. "He killed my mother to try and get to me."

Ash's confession was more than her heart could bear. She took a seat on the bed, eyes wide with shock. "Ash, I'm so sorry."

"It happened a long time ago," he said. But Rosalie could tell it was a wound that hadn't healed; would probably never heal.

"What does he want with the *variants*?"

"To use them to make his army stronger, if they'll join him. But our information suggests that, if they refuse…" He stopped short of completing his thought.

"What? What happens if they refuse?"

Ash considered sugar-coating it, but he also wanted her to understand. "Our intel suggests those who refuse to join him are kept in cages in a lab. He studies them, takes involuntary blood and tissue samples, even goes so far as to…" He took a breath.

"To what?" she asked impatiently.

"To experiment on them like animals," he blurted out indelicately. "He's trying to create a being with ultimate powers."

Rosalie's stomach churned at the thought of entire villages being slaughtered and people like her being treated as lab rats.

"That's why we go into the villages first. Our hope is that if the village doesn't harbor any *variants*, that Zebadiah and his army will leave the people alone."

Rosalie felt terrible for the loss Ash had endured. But she was also a firm believer that being wronged didn't justify wrong behavior. "Admit it, you also want to use those powers for your benefit."

"For the benefit of everyone," Ash corrected. "Our mission is to destroy Zebadiah and all his followers. Our army is undersized. We need all the help we can get."

Rosalie felt rocked as she tried to take it all in.

Ash continued. "Our plan isn't to kill anyone. In fact, my men call themselves the Liberation Alliance. We're trying to protect as many as we can, but we're also trying to win a war here."

"You should be open about your plans." What she didn't tell him, was she wanted him to be more open with her. It stung to realize how little he confided in her.

He was silent as he contemplated her last statement. "We have a Discerner in our group," he finally said. "He's able to both see and analyze several versions of the future. His visions indicate mostly negative consequences if we reveal too much of our plan too early. There are misunderstandings. Information leaks."

"You should have told *me*," she clarified. Her throat felt tight and her voice shook with emotion.

"I was trying to protect you from the truth."

"What truth? That instead of being your prisoner, I would have been someone else's?" It was below the belt, and she knew it. But she was angry for being kept in the dark.

"And how does knowing all of this help now? Does it make it more palatable to be with the likes of me?"

Waves of guilt and sadness hit her at once. She felt shame for the words she'd spoken in anger, but that didn't negate his actions or lack of openness. Uncertain how to respond, she crossed her arms in front of her chest and sat in stony silence.

Ash sighed deeply. He knelt beside the bed and took her hands in his. "Roe, there are specific reasons I couldn't tell you."

His words wounded her and she wondered if she'd misjudged their relationship. She leaned in closer, choosing her words carefully and trying to keep the emotion out of her voice. "Ash, what are you still not telling me?"

He shook his head. He couldn't tell her. It wouldn't bear fruit – only fear and resentment. He couldn't let her know about all the times Marx shared his visions of Rosalie's death; and that despite his visions, Ash had taken her from Mabel Village anyway. There was no good way to tell her that, no matter how he tried to change things, or how hard he tried to protect her, the Discerner repeatedly witnessed her demise.

CHAPTER EIGHTEEN

"Who are we going to meet again?" Rosalie was doing her best to keep up with Ash's long strides. She smiled to herself. Although she knew there were still things he hadn't shared, and was confused where they were headed, she was grateful he was including her in more of his plans.

"Jrynton. A recent recruit but I knew him a bit when we were younger. He's a Gifter."

"Ooh," she said, awestruck. "I've heard of those. They have no other power except to amplify the gifts of others around them. Such a selfless power. I've heard it said Gifters have the purest souls."

"Uh huh," Ash nodded, hiding a smirk as he knocked on the Gifter's door.

"Fike and fire," a man shouted from the other side of the door. A string of curse words followed before a middle-aged, blonde man opened the door, towering above Rosalie and Ash. He stood about seven feet tall and glared down at the pair with his coal black eyes. "What in the name of Helstice do you want?"

"Purest of souls?" Ash teased, looking at Rosalie. Then he turned to the man and said, "Good to see you, Jrynton."

"You look old," Jrynton told him. Then his handsome face split into a wide grin. He pulled Ash in for a bear hug, slapping him hard on the back. "Come in. Come in."

"So, you're a Mender and a Soother, huh?" he asked, addressing Rosalie.

She smiled and cleared her throat. "Yes, that's correct."

The man took her hand in his, pumping it vigorously. "It's nice to meet you." He raised an eyebrow and gave her a sideways look. "But not a Healer, eh?"

"Afraid not."

He rubbed his chin. "Hmm, curious."

"Why?" Ash asked.

Jrynton paused, as if he wanted to say something, but chose not to. "No reason. Let's see what we can do with the powers you do have, eh?"

Rosalie smiled. "I'm ready."

"First I want to see what you've got. Do we have someone we can experiment on?" He asked the question of Ash.

"I can probably find someone." Ash hesitated, his eyes darting towards the door, then back at Jrynton, who was staring intently at Rosalie.

"Relax, I'll behave myself," Jrynton teased.

Rosalie blushed, but not as deeply as Ash. "I wasn't thinking that."

"Sure you weren't."

"I'll go find someone. Try to be the pure soul Rosalie thought you were before she met you."

Rosalie rolled her eyes and Jrynton let out a hearty chuckle.

When Ash returned, he brought two men with him. "Kyron has an injured collarbone. And Spencer here got his foot stepped on by one of the horses."

Rosalie looked from Kyron to Spencer, then to Ash. "Going easy on me, huh?" she winked.

"Let's begin," Jrynton said.

Rosalie stroked Kyron's collarbone and began her mending and soothing routine. As she worked, Jrynton stood beside her and placed a firm hand on her shoulder.

"Concentrate," he said, giving her shoulder a squeeze.

She closed her eyes and felt an unusual surge of power. Her fingertips tingled. It was a warming sensation.

"That's it," he encouraged.

She continued to caress the injury, humming softly to herself without realizing it. She could feel the warmth from her fingers transfer to Kyron's skin, relieving his tension. The Gifter gave her shoulder another squeeze, and once again she felt a surge of power. She murmured a soothing chant as she swept her hand across Kyron's collarbone one final time. When she felt his pain subside, she opened her eyes and took a step back.

"That feels amazing," Kyron said. He rotated his shoulder and pressed his fingertips into his collarbone. "I don't feel any pain."

"You'll want to take it easy for a bit," Rosalie warned. "My powers make it feel better than it actually is. As a reminder, I'm not a Healer."

Kyron nodded.

For reasons that escaped the others, Jrynton smirked. Then, recovering quickly, he turned to Spencer. "Let's take a look at that foot next, shall we?"

CHAPTER NINETEEN

Rosalie knew Jrynton was helping the *variants* of the Liberation Alliance hone their powers, but she was surprised when she saw him talking to Talon from across the courtyard. Talon's face was drawn in concentration and he appeared to be focusing hard on whatever instruction Jrynton was providing. When Talon looked her way, she quickly averted her eyes and hurried in the opposite direction.

"Has Talon decided to join you?" she asked Ash later that day.

He flinched. It was the first time since Talon betrayed her that he'd heard Rosalie mention his name. It bothered him somehow. "We selected some of the stronger recruits to start training for combat. Only if they agreed, of course. But once we revealed our plans to take down Lord Zebadiah, most wanted to be a part of it. Talon volunteered. Stryker's training him in combat. Jrynton's training him to strengthen his powers."

The news took Rosalie by surprise. Not that Talon was asked to fight, but that he agreed. "I think I'd like to talk to him and try and mend things between us."

"Why? What do you see in that guy? He seems like such a weasel."

"He's my friend," she defended.

"He betrayed you." Ash's eyes flashed in anger and his jaw tightened.

"I owe him." Subconsciously she touched her hand to her shoulder blade and traced her scar with her fingertips.

Ash nodded, softening. He thought he finally understood. "I'll arrange it."

Rosalie felt a surge of happiness at seeing her old friend again. She'd missed him more than she'd realized. "How have you been?"

"As good as can be expected." His response was guarded.

She nodded and her throat tightened. It was the first time she could recall things being awkward between them. It made her heart hurt. "Look Talon, I'm really sorry. I understand why you did what you did."

"Stop," he broke in. "There's no excuse for what I did. You don't know how much I hate myself for it." His soft, brown eyes misted, making him look vulnerable.

"Let's both agree to forget it, how about that?"

He grinned. "I've missed you, Roe. How have you been, really?"

She took a breath. "Conflicted, to be honest. But good."

"You love him, don't you?"

She paused.

"It's okay, you can tell me."

"I do," she admitted without further hesitation.

Talon nodded. He didn't pass judgement. "Want to hear something strange?"

"What?"

"I love what I'm doing here – training for the Liberation Alliance. Once Stryker explained the cause to me, I knew I wanted to be a part of it."

"That's great, Talon." Her voice hitched. She was happy for him, but she felt sad. Worried. For all of them. She remembered her nightmare; remembered watching Talon die.

"Hey, it's going to be okay," he told her. "We're the good guys. We'll prevail."

She nodded again and smiled. But inside, she wasn't so sure. They still invaded villages; took people against their will. Did the end justify the means? For her the question remained: *were they the good guys?*

CHAPTER TWENTY

The ambush of the Liberation Alliance base camp came out of nowhere. No one could have predicted it, not even Marx. The attack took place before the dawn broke – which meant most of the men in the camp were unarmed; many still asleep. The invaders were dishonorable but inexperienced, seeking only to loot the camp and run away with its spoils. After the initial surprise, the trained Alliance overpowered the disorganized bandits, but not before injuries were suffered on both sides.

The front office was converted into a makeshift infirmary. Rosalie offered her soothing and mending powers to the mild and moderately injured. She left the more serious cases to the trained medics. Those injuries were beyond her skills.

She was tending to a man with superficial cuts on his hands and forearms when another man ran up to her, hollering and flailing his arms.

"Slow down, take a breath," Rosalie told him. "I can't understand what you're saying."

The man took a deep breath and spoke slowly – but his tone remained elevated. "Stryker asked for you right away."

Doing her best to keep up, Rosalie followed him as he sprinted towards the outer courtyard. She repeatedly murmured a short prayer to the gods that Ash was okay. When she rounded the corner to the stables, she was relieved, then horrified, to find it was Stryker's brother, Dillinger, lying on the ground. When she got closer, she could see he was bleeding heavily from a gaping wound in his abdomen.

Stryker was kneeling beside his brother, doing his best to stop the blood flow with the pressure of his hands. Ash and Jrynton were standing close by, looking helpless. When Rosalie approached, Stryker looked up at her and shot her a pleading look. His tone and expression seemed to say, while he never believed she belonged there, at this moment he was begging her to prove him wrong.

"You're a Healer," he cried out in desperation. "Do something."

"I'm a Soother and a Mender," Rosalie corrected him. "I can sooth the mind into thinking there isn't any pain. I can also speed up the body's natural mending process. But I can't heal. If wounds are fatal, there's nothing I can do but sooth the pain until the inevitable happens."

"So, you can't save him?" Ash asked. He stepped towards her and placed a comforting hand on her shoulder.

Filled with sadness and regret, she said, "I'm afraid not."

"I don't believe you," Stryker hissed, jumping to his feet and taking a step towards her. His eyes grew dark and his self-control wavered, his blood-soaked hands fisting at his sides.

Ash stepped in between them. "She isn't lying."

- 131 -

"And how would you know?" Stryker shrieked. His tone oozed with anger and fear. "She's got you so twisted up inside, you don't know if you're coming or going."

Ash channeled his patience. It angered him that Stryker thought Rosalie made him weak. "I've seen her powers, Stryker. She's not a Healer."

Jrynton interrupted, speaking calmly. "Rosalie, sweetheart, why don't you give it a try?"

"It's not fair to put that sort of pressure on her," Ash argued.

"I'll try," Rosalie spoke up. When the three men stared back at her, she said, "I'll see what I can do."

"Roe, you don't have to…" Ash began, but she ignored him.

She sank to her knees next to Dillinger. Jrynton placed a firm hand on her shoulder, encouraging her. "I'll help you," he said.

She looked up at him, nodded, then returned her attention to Dillinger. His chest heaved as he struggled to breathe. She wiped the sweat from his forehead and leaned in, speaking softly into his ear. "Neme lasomin, talikent – amnabe."

Dillinger moaned in pain. "What kind of sorcery are you trying to pull?" Stryker barked.

"Let her work," Ash and Jrynton said in unison.

Disregarding all of them, Rosalie concentrated on her patient. Her great-grandmother had been a Healer, and it was rumored the genetic anomaly could lay dormant for generations. But Rosalie had never tried to channel or hone the powers of a Healer. Far too many had been persecuted for such powers. When she was old enough, she'd learned her own great-grandmother had been burned as a witch – by some of

- 132 -

the very townsfolk she'd healed. People were frightened of what they didn't understand.

She worried Ash might think differently of her if she wielded all she might be capable of. But she couldn't think of that now. She could only think of saving the man who lay bleeding and dying in front of her.

"Neme lasomin, talikent – amnabe," she repeated. She pressed her hands over the wound and closed her eyes in deep concentration. She felt a slow burn. It started in her fingertips and spread to her hands. As she continued her caress, chanting all the while, the burning sensation intensified until she felt like her hands were on fire. The heat crept to her wrists and up her arms. The man beneath her groaned.

"She's killing him," Stryker growled. He paced, wringing his hands.

"She's doing great," Jrynton said.

Ash remained silent, taking it all in. A silent war raged inside him. *Should he stop her?*

Rosalie's eyes glistened and her cheeks were pink. Her expression was trance-like; haunted. She looked both fierce and vulnerable. The pain was becoming unbearable and tears fell from her eyes as she continued to chant. She wanted to move her hands but knew it might prove fatal to the man whose life depended on her powers. When her tears fell to the man's skin, she watched the teardrops sizzle and the man's wound closed ever so slightly. She began to rub his skin vigorously, allowing the pain she felt to summon her healing tears.

By now she was crying uncontrollably as the pain intensified. If she could only hold out a little longer. The ground beneath her swayed and a loud roaring sounded in her ears, followed by Dillinger's haunting screams. Or perhaps the screams came from her own lips. She knew she was losing consciousness – and if that happened, it likely meant she'd failed.

When Rosalie came to, she was lying in bed in Ash's room, above the covers, but Ash was nowhere around. She looked down at her bandaged hands. Her skin felt aflame. Someone had done their best to clean her up, but dried blood coated her arms and stained her clothes.

There was a soft knock at the door, and Stryker entered the room.

Rosalie struggled to sit up in bed, terrified. *Had he come to finish her off since she'd failed to save his brother?*

"Stryker, I'm so sorry," she began.

"Shh. Rosalie. It's me who should be apologizing. You were amazing. I have you to thank for saving my brother's life."

She blinked twice, processing his words. "You mean, he's alive?" She was overcome with relief.

Stryker's face split into a wide grin. It softened his features. "You didn't know? He's not only alive, he's out there having dinner with the men."

She began to cry. Mostly happy tears, but she also worried what people would think of her – or do to her – now that everyone realized she was a Healer. She was having trouble coming to grips with it herself.

"Are you hurting?" Stryker asked, the inflection in his tone revealing his obvious discomfort. He wasn't used to dealing with such raw emotion.

"Just a little bit. Sorry, I guess I'm just coming to terms with everything."

He smiled appreciatively at her and patted her arm. "You really didn't know you had it in you, did you?"

She shook her head *no*. "Is Ash mad?" she blurted out.

"Why would he be mad?"

"I don't want him to think I hid anything from him." With the mounds of pillows and blankets surrounding her delicate frame, and her wide, pleading eyes, she looked fragile. "Stryker, I honestly didn't know."

"If Ash is anything, he's beyond proud of you. And worried," he said, touching the bandages on her hands.

A smile spread across her lips. Her shoulders sank into the pillows in relief. "My great-grandmother was a Healer," she explained. "People weren't very kind to her when they found out. I'm afraid it didn't end well for her."

"All the men here will keep you safe," he assured her. "What you did was brave, and I am eternally grateful."

Jrynton filed in next.

"You knew," Rosalie said, realizing it for the first time.

"That you were a Healer?"

She nodded.

His eyes crinkled. "I had a feeling. When I shook your hand, I sensed the power that passed between us was stronger than that of a Mender or a Soother."

"Why didn't you tell me?"

"I also sensed something was holding you back from accepting your power."

Rosalie nodded but didn't offer an explanation.

"Want a little free advice?"

She smiled. "I'd love some."

"Never underestimate yourself," he told her. "And never be afraid to explore who you really are." He leaned in and planted a chaste kiss on her cheek. "And never stop wearing whatever that intoxicating perfume is you're wearing," he teased before taking his leave.

Laughing and shaking her head, she mumbled to herself, "Purest soul."

Ash entered the room shortly after Jrynton left. "You're awake," he said.

Rosalie smiled shyly at him. He walked to the bedside and lifted one of her bandaged hands to his lips.

"Can you heal yourself?"

She shook her head *no*. "Unfortunately, my powers don't work like that. I can't self-soothe, and I can't mend or heal myself."

He'd already known the answer. His powers never worked on himself either. But he hated to see her in pain.

"The skin isn't broken or blistered," he told her. "Only red. We put some cream on it."

"It will heal in a few days. I'm told my great-grandmother's hands used to do the same thing."

"I'm proud of you, Roe," he admitted. "You saved a good man today."

She stared up at him. He appeared sad. A lock of his red hair fell on his forehead, and he brushed it back with his forearm.

"I promise I didn't hold out on you," she said, worried she was the reason for his sadness. "I really didn't know." Although she wondered to herself if subconsciously, she always knew.

Ash leaned in and kissed her forehead. "It isn't that. I was having selfish thoughts."

"Oh?" she teased.

"Well, until now people assumed you were just some girl I was using for amusement. And I was fine letting them think that, because they left us alone. But now that they've seen your powers…"

"You're worried they'll want more from me," she finished for him. He nodded.

"I thought the same thing," she admitted.

The room fell quiet. Rosalie thought about what Jrynton had told her. *Never be afraid to explore who you really are.*

"I want to tell you about my scar now," she said, breaking the silence.

"You sure?"

She nodded and Ash stretched out next to her on the bed. She began to tell him about how her great-grandmother had been tortured and burned once the villagers discovered her healing powers. She explained how she had kept her soothing and mending powers a secret, even from her closest friends. "When I was sixteen, a classmate was injured during a game of stick-splat ball. You remember, the game where you hold the stick…"

"I remember it," Ash interrupted. He knew she was stalling.

Rosalie drew out a breath, then continued. "Anyway, I could tell his arm was busted and he was screaming in pain. I didn't think. I

- 137 -

rushed over to him and performed a soothing chant until the medical team arrived to take him away." By now tears streamed down her pretty face, but she continued. "After school I was walking home through the woods, alone, and three of the boy's friends jumped me. They taunted me, called me a witch and accused me of putting a curse on their friend." Her shoulders shook.

Ash pulled her close. "Roe, you can stop now if you need to."

"No, I need to talk it through." She wiped her eyes with the back of her bandaged hands and took another labored breath. "One boy shoved me. I lost my balance and fell to my knees. He kicked me in the back and shoved my face into the dirt. Another boy must have had a lighter or a match. He'd lit the end of a branch on fire and he kept screaming that I needed to burn. He tore my shirt and shoved the burning stick into my shoulder blade."

Ash wanted to tell her to stop. He couldn't bear to hear anymore. But it would be selfish not to let her continue. Instead he sat up in bed and scooped her into his lap, cradling her in his arms. "Go on, Roe," he heard himself say.

"They were ripping at my clothes, pulling my hair, and saying all sorts of foul things... and that's when Talon saved me. He came up on the scene and charged at all three boys. He knocked one senseless and the other two ran away. I had an ugly scar to show for it, but it could have been so much worse."

Story complete, she snuggled closer to him and felt comfort in his warmth. Silent tears of healing fell from her face. Lost for words, Ash stroked her hair and rocked her like a child. He made a mental note to find better living arrangements for Talon. Petty jealousies aside, he owed the man a great deal of gratitude.

"Your scar isn't ugly," he said aloud.

Rosalie laughed despite herself. "You have this way of saying all the wrong things, and yet somehow, it's exactly what I need to hear."

Ash chuckled. He leaned down and kissed her.

"I've never shared that story with anyone else. Not even my parents. Only Talon and those three boys know about it. Now, someday you'll tell me your deepest and darkest secret." She gazed up at him expectedly.

He nodded. "I will," he said, and they both pretended to believe it.

CHAPTER TWENTY-ONE

Rosalie heard Ash's army singing from afar off. She'd been pacing the floors for over an hour, anxiously awaiting their safe return. When she heard the men approaching, the knots in her stomach loosened. The closer the men came, the louder and more off-key they sounded. She would have found it comical if she hadn't been so concerned about their safety.

I told her a lie, and kissed her goodbye,
Never to find my way home.

She recognized the lyrics as an old bar tune and her concern was replaced with annoyance. She'd been sick with worry and here they were … drunken and celebrating.

The tromping of Ash's feet, followed by muffled cursing when he lost his balance, officially announced his arrival outside their shared room. When Rosalie flung open the door, he stumbled through it.

"Where have you been?" she asked, hands on her hips.

He offered her a sheepish grin. The scent of gin lingered on his breath.

"You're drunk."

"No, baby, I just had a little."

"It doesn't smell like just a little."

When he started to argue, he pitched forward and she caught him by the arm. "Here, let me help you into bed."

"Will you be joining me?" he asked, obnoxiously.

"Absolutely not." She helped him into bed, then removed his boots. When she bent down to straighten the covers, he grabbed her wrist and held it.

"I was too late. I couldn't save them," he whispered.

He'd slurred his words and Rosalie wondered if she'd misheard him. Before she could ask, he passed out.

Once they'd sobered up, Ash, Stryker, and the Discerner met behind closed doors to discuss the disaster they'd encountered the day before. By the time the Liberation Alliance had arrived at the village, it was a devastating site. Most of the homes had been burned to the ground. There was death and destruction everywhere. There were no survivors. Even the livestock had been slaughtered. Ash knew it was the work of Lord Zebadiah, ruler of Castle Druin. It churned his stomach.

His men had taken it hard, especially the ones without prior battle experience. He recalled the way Skatson, barely nineteen, had thrown up at the scene. Some of the men wept openly.

It had been Stryker's idea to go to the local bar. The townspeople wouldn't be needing it. Without a bartender to fix their drinks – or regulate them – things had gotten out of hand fast; but it was the perfect way to blow off steam. Liquid therapy.

"What happened out there yesterday?" Ash asked the Discerner. His tone wasn't accusatory. He was still shell-shocked by the previous day's events.

Marx sat silent for a moment. "Lord Zebadiah must have changed his plans. My visions indicated his Receptor wouldn't recommend that village for weeks. They must know what we're up to, and they're making adjustments."

"How were you not able to see it?"

"I have two theories. They might both be the reason, actually."

"Let's hear them."

"First, Lord Zebadiah must not be making a decision on what village to hit until shortly before the raid. If a decision isn't made, there's nothing for me to foresee."

Stryker looked thoughtful.

Ash looked doubtful. "And the second reason?"

"My visions have been fuzzy since we invaded Mabel Village."

Ash became defensive. "Are you suggesting Rosalie's the cause?"

"Actually, no. The man who came from the same village as her."

"Talon?" Stryker asked. There was disappointment in his voice. He had accepted Talon as somewhat of a protégé.

"There's something about him. I can't get a read on him; and as I said, ever since he arrived, my powers feel dulled. Unreliable."

A thought occurred to Ash and he felt guilty he hadn't considered it before. "He's a Blocker," he revealed.

"He mentioned that," Stryker said, "but I wasn't quite sure what it meant."

"From what I understand, he can block people's powers from working on him. And he can extend that power to block people from inflicting their power on others he comes in contact with."

Marx paused to consider this information. "I don't think he's intentionally blocking my visions. My guess is his powers are stronger than he realizes. Perhaps under duress or unfamiliar circumstances, he's doing more blocking than he intends to."

"Well, that's easy then," Stryker said. "We cut our losses. He's doing us more harm than good. We'll dump him at the next village."

"No," Ash cut in.

"No?" Stryker argued. "You just heard Marx say…"

"I mean, no, we owe him more than that."

"We don't owe him a th…"

"*I* owe him," Ash said. He didn't elaborate. The edge to his voice indicated there would be no debate. "I'll give him a horse, some supplies, and allow him to return to his village."

Marx and Stryker looked at each other, realizing there was no arguing.

"If that's what you think is best," Stryker said. But he didn't hide his annoyance as he stalked past Ash, jerked open the door, and slammed it shut behind him.

"Remember who's on your side here," Marx said. He placed a hand on Ash's shoulder. His kind eyes crinkled with concern. "As our leader, we trust your judgement. But don't forget the ones who helped you get here."

When Ash approached Talon about returning to his village, he left out the part about him blocking the Discerner's visions. He didn't want him to shoulder any of the guilt over not being able to prevent Lord Zebadiah's attack on the last village. Ash was weighed down with enough guilt for the two of them. He took a different approach.

"You want me to go back to Mabel Village to protect them?" Talon asked.

"Yes," Ash lied. "We have reason to believe Lord Zebadiah is still targeting your village. Perhaps we left a *variant* behind." He was improvising.

"If there is anyone besides me and Roe, they're either new, or they've done an incredible job of keeping their power a secret."

"Whatever the reason, I think it would be best if you returned to check it out."

When Talon hesitated, Ash said, "I know Rosalie is worried and thinks it's what's best."

"Roe asked that I go?"

Ash winced at the intimate use of Rosalie's nickname. He shouldn't feel jealous. Talon had been her friend for years; and had been using the nickname far before Ash even met Rosalie. But it was hard to hear all the same.

"Yes, she thought it was time. She wanted to return herself, but her powers are needed in case we encounter injuries." Although he was doing it for the greater good, Ash felt guilty for his deception.

"I will go then," Talon said decidedly. "I'd like to say goodbye to Roe first, if that's possible."

"I'm afraid time is of the essence. I'll pass along your goodbyes."

Talon looked disappointed but didn't argue. "Take good care of her then."

"I intend to," he said in earnest. The two men clasped arms, a respectful promise made, then Talon turned to go.

"I tried to find Talon earlier today," Rosalie said when she and Ash were alone.

Ash tensed beside her. "And?" he asked after a pause.

"And he wasn't there."

He exhaled, slowly. "I let him return to his village." He hoped it would be the end of it, though he knew Rosalie better than that.

"Why? Why wouldn't you tell me? Why wouldn't he say goodbye?"

"Talon asked to go back, so I sent him back. Now can we just drop this?"

"You lie," Rosalie said. The panic rose in her voice. "Something happened to him, didn't it? He joined your soldiers on the last raid and you got him killed. I know it." Her throat tightened, and her words sounded strangled.

"Roe, no..."

"I don't believe you. Does this have anything to do with why you and your men got drunk yesterday?"

He didn't answer.

"I can't. I can't stay here right now." Choking back tears, she ran from the room.

Ash let her go, assuming she needed time to cool off. He knew she sensed his deception, but it still angered him she immediately assumed the worst about him. Talon wasn't his favorite person, but he knew how Rosalie felt about him and for that he wouldn't have let anything happen to him. He thought he'd earned her trust. Perhaps he'd misjudged where he stood with her. Then again, he hadn't exactly been forthright about Talon's reasons for leaving. Maybe her distrust in him was deserved.

Tears streamed down Rosalie's face as she ran. She half expected Ash to run after her, but when she glanced behind her, he was nowhere in sight. She didn't realize she'd run in the direction of the horse stables until she arrived. It was the first place she thought of when she wanted to feel at peace. She approached her favorite horse, Raffey, the palomino. She fished a brush from a bucket and began to groom the horse the way Othelia taught her.

Her tears continued at a steady flow as she pulled the brush across the horse's beautiful mane. She didn't hear when her friend approached.

"What are you doing?" Othelia's chirpy voice spoke up from behind her.

Startled, Rosalie wiped her tears with the back of her hand, then turned to face her.

Othelia's cheerful smile vanished when she saw her friend's distress. "What's wrong?"

"Nothing," she lied, not wanting to speak ill of Ash, no matter how upset she was with him.

"It doesn't look like nothing."

Rosalie offered a wan smile. "Ash and I got in a small fight. It's fine."

Not wanting to pry, Othelia picked up another brush and joined in. The two women worked in silence for a better part of an hour before Rosalie spoke up again.

"Where's Charlie?"

"Charlie?"

"You know, the chestnut mare. Beautiful coloring." She offered a feeble smile. "Terrible attitude."

"Ash let one of the prisoners, err, recruits, have him."

Rosalie paused with her brush in mid-air. "He... he let someone have Charlie?"

"Yeah. I guess there was a recruit who needed to go back to his village. Ash agreed. Gave him a horse and everything. Let's see, what was the man's name? Tarlyn or something."

"Talon?" Hope welled up inside her.

"Yeah, that sounds right."

A surge of relief rushed through her. "Please excuse me." She dropped the grooming brush and raced back to her room.

"I'm an idiot," she said the moment she burst into the room. Her cheeks were flushed, more from shame than her brief run.

Ash was sitting in a chair in the corner, tying his shoes. He looked up and caught her gaze. He wanted to be angry, but he was too relieved she'd changed her mind about him. He also didn't want her to press him on his reasons for letting Talon leave. He forced a smile. "It's fine," he said.

She felt guilty. "No, it's not fine." She approached him slowly. "You did a great thing, and I accused you of something terrible."

When she was standing in front of him, she crouched down so she was eye level with him. "I'm really, really sorry."

He grinned and pulled her onto his lap, kissing her. "Forget it."

"So, what did happen yesterday?" she asked.

"I'm not sure I'm ready to talk about it."

Rosalie didn't press him. Relaxing her body, she rested her head on his shoulder. She knew he'd tell her in time. At least, she hoped he would.

CHAPTER TWENTY-TWO

"Did I see a female brought in?" Rosalie asked Ash upon his successful return from Grockdurn. She tried to sound casual.

"Yes. Lexis. But admittedly, she found us. When the gas didn't work on her, she marched straight up to us, told us she'd heard rumor of the Alliance's existence, and asked to join us. She's a Soother, actually, like you."

Ash was animated. It was obvious the woman impressed him.

"Explains why she's able to walk around so freely," Rosalie said. "And, like me, will she be staying with you?" As hard as she tried, she knew she failed to mask the jealousy and bitterness in her tone.

He rubbed his chin, as if considering. Rosalie's eyes narrowed and she held her breath.

Face splitting into a wide grin, he laughed. "Of course not. She's going to bunk with Othelia."

Relief washed over her, and her face brightened. "I mean, it would be okay if you wanted her to."

"You're a terrible liar." He pulled her in for a kiss and held her tight. For such a confident young woman, he was baffled by her bouts of insecurity.

When Lexis joined Rosalie in the laundry room that afternoon, Rosalie was determined to keep quiet. She didn't want to strike up a friendship with this woman. There were too many unknowns, too many variables.

The problem was, Lexis was hard not to like. She had a quick wit and a disarming sense of humor. In a camp full of men, and in contrast to Othelia's quiet, calm demeanor, Lexis was a refreshing change. Rosalie found herself warming to her. They swapped stories and laughs over a mountain of laundry.

"You ladies look like you're having a good time."

Rosalie turned to see who spoke. She didn't recognize the man who stood in the doorway. He was massive. With his flannel shirt and bushy beard, he looked like a lumberjack. He offered a toothy grin but something in his demeanor was off-putting.

"May we help you?" Rosalie asked. Her tone was unfriendly. She didn't want to encourage him.

The man ignored her and stared in Lexis' direction. "I heard Ash brought in a pretty, young thing." He licked his lips.

Lexis barely glanced up from the laundry she was folding. "Someone exaggerated."

"Not from where I'm standing." He stepped into the room, watching Lexis closely.

"What do you want?" Rosalie demanded, hands on her hips.

The man continued to ignore her. Lexis continued to pretend to be engrossed in folding the mound of clothes in front of her.

"I've been sent to keep an eye on you ladies. See if you need anything."

Rosalie profoundly doubted his statement. Her stomach churned when she realized she'd left her knife in her room when she'd changed clothes. Her eyes darted around the laundry room for something she could use as a weapon if matters got out of hand.

The man put his elbows on the counter, leaning towards Lexis. "You make folding laundry look sexy."

Lexis was doing her best to sidestep the man's advances, but Rosalie could tell she was getting nervous.

"If I take these clothes off right now, are you going to wash them for me?" The ill-mannered man slid his hand down his chest. He hooked his thumb in his beltloop and stared back at Lexis, as if he expected a response to his vulgar offer.

Lexis tried to keep the conversation light. "Now, now, is that any way to talk to a lady?" She moved to the farthest washer, putting some distance between her and the brute of a man.

It didn't work. He sidled up beside her and put a hand on her shoulder, trying to pull her closer.

She pushed him off. Rosalie squared her shoulders and prepared to jump in to aid her new friend. The man was a giant. She knew they were unevenly matched.

"You're a saucy little thing, aren't you?" He pulled Lexis close and clamped his lips on hers.

Lexis slapped him. Rosalie rushed forward.

Startled, the man grabbed his cheek and his face turned red as a beet. He raised his arm to backhand her.

Lexis lifted her arm in front of her face to defend herself. Rosalie knew she wouldn't get to her in time. She was doing her best to reach her when Ash spoke up from the doorway.

"My father thought it was okay to hit a woman too."

The chaos of the room came to a halt. Three heads whipped in Ash's direction. He stood tall and menacing. "I broke both his hands," he continued as he stepped into the room. "Made sure he never raised them to a woman again. Don't think I won't hesitate to do the same to you."

The man lowered his arm and stepped away from Lexis. "I'm sorry, sir."

"Don't apologize to me. It wasn't me you tried to strike." He arched an eyebrow.

The man turned towards Lexis. "I'm very sorry," he mumbled, then slunk from the room, shooting Ash a sideways look of apology as he left. Ash glared back. He'd deal with him later. There was no place in his camp for a man of so little character.

Lexis' breath came out in a whoosh of relief. She rushed to Ash's side and slung her slender arms around his neck. "Thank you," she said. Her tone sounded flirty, and Rosalie's hands involuntarily balled into fists at her sides. She had no right to be angry. Didn't she try to charm Ash herself when she first arrived?

Ash patted the woman twice on the back, then stepped out of the embrace. "It was nothing. You ladies let me know if you run into further trouble, okay?" Rosalie was surprised to see he was grinning at Lexis. Worse, he was flirting.

"Did you really beat up your own father?" Lexis asked, wide-eyed and grinning. She placed her hands on her curvy hips, playfully demanding an answer.

He flashed her a wicked grin. "Nah. My father left when I was nine. I haven't seen him since. But I was convincing, right?" When he shot Lexis a wink, Rosalie slammed the washer lid closed. Lexis jumped. Ash looked both surprised and amused.

"Thank you for *rescuing* us," Rosalie said. Her voice dripped with the sweetness of honey. Lexis may not have realized it, but Ash caught the sarcasm in her tone.

Maintaining his flirty smile, he said, "Well I'll leave you two to it then." He made a gesture of tipping his hat, though he wasn't wearing one, and left the room.

"He is dreamy," Lexis said breathily once she and Rosalie were alone.

Rosalie took a deep breath. It wasn't this woman's fault she took an immediate liking to Ash. Who wouldn't? "He is sort of cute, isn't he?" she said instead, trying to sound casual. Her insecurities resurfaced.

After dinner, Lexis trotted over to Rosalie, who stood stoking the campfire.

"I came here to apologize."

"For what?" She kept her eyes trained on the fire.

"I didn't realize you and Ash were together."

- 153 -

Rosalie tensed and her ears burned. She didn't look at Lexis. She continued to stare into the flames instead. "What makes you think we're together?"

"I saw the way the two of you gazed at each other over dinner."

"Sort of the way he stared at you in the laundry room." She tried to hide the jealousy in her tone.

Lexis laughed. It was a sweet, airy laugh. "Not even close to the same look."

Rosalie smiled and poked at the fire with a stick. Finally, she turned to Lexis and said, "There's really no need to apologize but thank you."

"Good. Now, what do you say we sneak back to the kitchen and see if we can whip up a dessert?"

Face brightening, Rosalie hooked arms with her new friend. "Okay, but we'd better make enough for Othelia too, or she may never forgive us."

CHAPTER TWENTY-THREE

When Rosalie rolled over in bed, she was surprised to find Ash still asleep beside her. She could tell by the amount of light streaming in the window that it was late morning. She'd overslept – and apparently, so had he.

Gently, she shook him awake. "No recruiting today?"

Since she'd gone with him to one of the villages, she chose her words carefully. She didn't want to offend him with terms like *raid* or *invasion*.

He rubbed his eyes, smiling at her word choice. "No recruiting?" Then he shot up in bed. "Shyde, we've slept in. Today's moving day."

"Moving day?" She sat up in bed and rested her back against the headboard.

"Sorry, Roe. It slipped my mind. We have one last base camp before we invade Castle Druin. From there I'll prepare my men with the training they need for battle."

Rosalie frowned, looking troubled.

"Hey, don't worry," he said, tucking a strand of hair behind her ear. "There'll still be hot showers at the new camp."

She slapped him playfully on the arm. "That is *not* what I'm worried about."

"I know," he said more seriously. "I promise you, Love, everything will be fine." He wished he felt as confident as he sounded. "I have one piece of good news," he said, changing the subject.

"What's that?"

"We've expanded our team of horses, so you'll be able to ride by yourself today."

"That is good news she said." But inside, she felt the tiniest pang of regret she wouldn't be riding double with him.

The Liberation Alliance was hours into the journey when Ash signaled his men to slow down. On the road ahead stood a family of three; their wagon parked partway in the road. The couple appeared to be in their mid-twenties; the little boy, no more than five. The front, right wheel of the family's wagon had busted and the couple was working desperately to repair it by themselves. But the weight of the wagon was too great for them to lift on their own.

Ash pulled back on the reins and held up one hand, motioning the men behind him to stop.

Stryker rode up on his right, bringing his horse to a halt beside him. "Why are we stopping?" he asked.

"This family needs help."

Stryker rolled his eyes. "You and your bleeding heart." But he wasn't angry – only amused.

"If we get them off the road, we'll have a larger pathway for the men to cross."

"Uh huh."

Ash grinned. "Fine, I'm a big softie." He dismounted and walked his horse over to Rosalie, handing her the reins. She took the reins while trying to settle her own horse.

"You're not going to have one of the men do it?" Stryker called out.

"You're one of the men," Ash yelled over his shoulder, still grinning.

Stryker mumbled something under his breath before dismounting and joining his friend.

Rosalie watched with curiosity and admiration as Ash approached the timid family. He extended his hand and the husband shook it hesitantly while the wife nervously rung her hands. Rosalie imagined the army of men must make an intimidating sight. Ash said a few words and ruffled the little boy's hair as he spoke. Whatever he said, it put the family at ease. He motioned for a few of his men to help. Three of his men lifted the wagon while Stryker and Ash worked to slide the spare wheel onto the axle. The wheel put up a fight before it clicked into place.

Ash circled around to the back of the wagon and retrieved a small bucket of tar. Sweat lined his hairline as he again squatted beside the wagon. His brow furrowed in concentration as he used the tar to grease the wheel, then double-checked that the hub was secure. He wiped his greasy hands on his shorts as he stood to his feet. "That oughta do it."

The husband thanked him with a handshake. The wife thanked him with a kiss on the cheek. Rosalie's eyes flashed with jealousy. She knew Ash couldn't help the way women responded to him, but she didn't have to like it. She turned the reins over to him with a huff. He offered her a sheepish grin and a wink. She melted in response. With every selfless act she witnessed, she fell further in love with him.

The new base camp was a dream – a luxurious mansion wrapped in brilliant, white stone. Walking paths surrounded the estate, twisting into entryways, outbuildings, and luscious gardens. Ash led his men to an impressive stable located to the right of the stately home. A small crew of stable hands welcomed the group, unphased by their presence.

Taking Rosalie by the hand, Ash led her down the walkway to the front of the house while he left his men to see to it that the horses were squared away. He knocked on the entryway door, paused for a beat, then fished a spare key from a nearby flowerpot.

"Wow, secure," Rosalie laughed.

Ash grinned back at her, then unlocked the door and pushed it open.

The elaborate foyer took her breath away. The entryway boasted travertine floors, grand chandeliers etched in gold, and a marble statue carved in the likeness of a tall, powerful-looking man.

"Who lives here?" Rosalie said in awe as she took it all in.

"We do. Or at least, we own it. It's headquarters for the Liberation Alliance. It was bequeathed to us by a wealthy patron who believed in our cause."

"It's magnificent."

"Yeah, we call it home," Ash said, shrugging his shoulders. He winked at Rosalie as he took her by the hand and led her to a nearby staircase. "The estate includes a team of roughly twenty caretakers for the home, livestock, and the grounds."

"Impressive."

Ash gave her a tour of the mansion with it spacious, fully furnished rooms. "Is one of these rooms reserved for us?" she asked seductively, raising an eyebrow.

"You don't waste any time, do you?" he teased.

She wanted to tell him she wanted to take advantage of any time they had left, but that fact would make them both sad. Instead she told him, "I'm going to take a bath, if you'd like to join me."

He led her to the nearest master suite. He figured, with his men busy unpacking, his absence would go unnoticed for a bit.

Ash slipped out of the room, leaving Rosalie sleeping soundly between the fine, satin sheets of the king-sized bed. He made his way down the corridor, to the room at the far end of the hallway. When he rapped his knuckles on the door three times, he heard the turn of the lock and the chain being slid from the door.

The silver-haired Discerner opened the door, looking bleary eyed and tired.

"Has there been a change?" Ash asked, not giving the man a chance to speak.

"Come in," Marx said.

Ash sat on the edge of the bed and his silver-haired friend took a seat in the corner chair. "Give it to me straight, Marx."

"There's been a change," he admitted. "Your victory is almost certain."

Ash offered a half smile. "But?"

The Discerner took a labored breath. "I can no longer foresee what happens to the girl."

"What does that mean?" Ash asked, straightening his spine.

"I'm not certain. I think it means there are too many variables. I'm afraid I can't say one way or the other if she'll be safe."

"That could be good news then, right? I mean, this time you didn't see her..." He couldn't bring himself to say the words. He'd heard accounts of Rosalie's death more times than he cared to remember. At first it was no more than an inevitable, unfortunate story. Now the thought pained him and was unthinkable.

"Again, I can't be certain. There are no guarantees."

"Then she doesn't come."

"I've explained this to you. My visions all indicate her presence at the battle is crucial to your victory."

"But again, you're not certain."

Marx nodded reluctantly.

"Then she doesn't come." He spoke each word slowly, with purpose.

Marx knew when Ash made up his mind, there was no arguing. "I'll let you know if that decision changes anything."

Ash nodded and stood to his feet. He left the room, the words of the Discerner weighing heavy on his mind. And soul.

Rosalie awoke to a tapping on her bedroom door. The early morning light was streaming through the window. Ash had left her about an hour before to join his men for their morning training regimen. While wiping the sleep from her eyes, she wondered if he forgot something – though she was curious why he'd knock.

She crept to the door and peered through the peephole. An elderly gentleman with long, silvery hair and a wiry beard stood outside her door. His face was etched in hard lines and stippled with liver spots, but his eyes were kind – wise and enchanting. He didn't frighten her. Curious, she opened the door a crack.

"May I help you?" she asked.

As usual, there was a man seated in the hallway outside her door, guarding it. Only now the sentry was there to protect her, not keep her from escaping. The sentry appeared unalarmed by the old man's presence at such an early hour.

"My name is Marx," the man told her. "I'm a Discerner. May I come in?"

CHAPTER TWENTY-FOUR

The preparation for battle was in full swing. Ash, Stryker, and Dillinger walked from soldier to soldier, providing instruction to the newer recruits on the lunge, the proper way to hold a sword, and how to effectively sidestep an attack. Once Ash revealed his plans, all but a handful of *variants* had agreed to join his cause. Most were eager to avenge loved ones or be part of a greater good. Those who didn't want to join willingly were released to be reunited with their villages (though they would have to find their own way). Ash revealed that for the remaining weeks, he and his men would concentrate their efforts on preparing for battle rather than gaining new recruits.

While much of the Liberation Alliance were seasoned soldiers who'd been in their share of battles, many others were young, inexperienced, and required considerable instruction. And patience.

When Ash noticed Rosalie intently watching his men from her perch on the split-rail fence, he grinned and walked over to her. It pleased him to see her taking such an interest in the training.

"They're doing well," she observed.

He grunted. "Some more than others. Some are … Shyde Roe, some are barely older than babies."

"Do you think they'll be ready in time?"

"They'll have to be. The harvest season is coming. We can't wait much longer."

"You will lead them," she said confidently.

"Luckily I have Stryker. He's a good instructor. More patient than me."

"Somehow, I find that hard to believe."

Ash grinned at her. "That is true. Someone has been teaching me a great deal of patience lately." When she smiled back at him, he tucked a strand of hair behind her ear. Then, without hesitation, he leaned in and kissed her on the mouth.

Rosalie gently pushed him away, startled. "Won't your men care?" She looked around to see who'd witnessed their exchange.

He shrugged. "They're going to have to get used to it." Then he pulled her closer, kissing her again. This time she didn't resist. She closed her eyes, blocking out the world around her, and returned his kiss with equal fervor.

In the days that passed, the soldiers continued to prepare for battle, but Ash was worried. Plunging swords into old flour sacks filled with straw would do nothing to prepare his men for the way it felt to sink a blade into human flesh; the way it changed a person. He still remembered his first kill. No matter how justified, the memory of watching the light go out of the man's eyes and witnessing him draw his last breath would always haunt him. He stared into the wide eyes of his younger recruits and was staggered by a sudden surge of guilt.

"They'll be fine," Stryker spoke up from behind him.

Ash turned to him; the worry sketched across his handsome face. "Were we ever this green?"

"Nah," Stryker said, giving his friend an affectionate pat on the back. "We were worse."

Once Ash realized his men would need more development than he could offer, he called upon Jrynton for his services. As a Gifter, Jrynton not only amplified the powers of the *variants* by touching them, he also instructed them on the ways to hone their powers through meditation and exercise. Each morning he instructed a class to prepare the *variants* for presenting their best selves during the upcoming battle.

"Why do we have to do this so bloody early?" Stryker complained.

"Jrynton insists that's when everyone is most adaptable," Ash explained. "Personally, I think he does it to torture us."

Stryker chuckled and lined up next to his men.

"Eyes forward," Jrynton barked. "Today we're going to concentrate on breathing patterns."

The group groaned in unison.

"This will be a valuable tool," the Gifter explained. "Your powers are most dominant when you're focused – alert."

From her usual perch on the fence, Rosalie watched in amusement as Jrynton forced the men into various poses and breathing exercises. She couldn't help but wonder if he was messing with them a bit. As a *variant* herself, she understood the importance of remaining focused –

but she failed to see how crouching in the dirt with one leg extended towards the heavens would help center anyone.

When Jrynton looked up, and caught her watching him, he grinned and shot her a conspiratorial wink. She grinned back at him; her suspicions confirmed.

CHAPTER TWENTY-FIVE

When Ash opened the bedroom door, Rosalie was crawling around on all fours and muttering like a crazy person.

"What are you doing?"

She glanced up at him, then continued crawling on the floor while sweeping her hands across the carpeting. "I lost my necklace," she explained.

"When did you see it last?"

"I don't know." Her tone was frustrated.

"Let me help you." He dropped to his knees beside her. The pair felt along the trim and the doorway. They searched under the bed and beneath the settee, but the necklace was nowhere to be found.

Rosalie's back was turned to him, but Ash could see her shoulders start to shake. He crawled towards her and she climbed into his lap, wrapping her legs around his waist and burying her head in his chest. There he held her while she cried. Deep sobs racked her body as he tried in vain to comfort her. She wept because the necklace was the only thing she had left from home. She wept because she missed Talon; missed her village. She wept for the uncertainty of her future – her future with Ash. She wept bitter tears for all the things she thought she couldn't share.

"It's not just about the necklace," she finally choked out through her sobs.

"I know baby," he whispered, smoothing her hair away from her face. He planted a kiss on her forehead and cradled her face in his hands. "I know."

After considerable coaxing and two fingers of homebrewed bourbon, Rosalie finally fell asleep. Ash, however, was wide awake. He hated to see her so torn up. He knew it wasn't just about the necklace. She'd been through a great deal in such a short period and she had a lot to process. Perhaps he'd been selfish not to send her back to her village with Talon. He stroked her cheek with the back of his hand. Her skin felt soft, warm.

He leaned in to kiss her. First her cheek, then her neck. When he placed his lips to her skin, where her necklace once was, he had an idea. Slowly, quietly, he crawled out of bed.

When Rosalie awoke, a small headache was forming between her eyes and at the base of her skull. She figured it was the crying, or the bourbon – perhaps both. She pressed her thumb and index finger to the space between her eyes, hoping to dull the pain.

"I've got something for you," she heard Ash whisper beside her.

She rolled over to face him. He was sitting up in bed, bare-chested, covers pulled up to his waist, and dangling a shiny object from his fingertips.

"My necklace." She shot straight up in bed; headache forgotten. A smile spread across her face and her eyes twinkled with delight.

Ash nodded and handed it to her.

"Where did you find it?" she asked as she slipped the necklace around her neck and fiddled with the clasp.

"In the laundry room. In the bottom of a wash machine, to be exact."

"That's right. I remember now. I slipped it into my pants pocket before my bath. I must have thrown those pants in the wash."

Ash nodded again.

"Ash, you're a genius."

He grinned. "I have my moments."

"I love you," she told him, flinging her arms around his neck.

"And I just want you to be happy." He took her hand in his and pressed it to his lips. He searched her eyes for any trace of the heartache he'd witnessed the night before.

"You make me happy," she told him.

His brow furrowed with concern and he stroked her cheek with the back of his hand. "Tell me how I can make you happier."

"You honestly couldn't do more. I just don't want to lose you. To lose us."

"Roe, that will never happen."

She took him by the hand. "Nothing is certain," she whispered.

"How I feel about you is." He unbuttoned her nightshirt and let his hands explore her body, admiring the rise and fall of her chest. He pushed her shirt off her shoulders and his mouth found her breasts. She sucked in her breath and tilted her head backwards, closing her eyes.

Her hands rested on his bare chest, then traveled below the covers. She was surprised to find he was already naked. "Someone was certain finding my necklace would be rewarded," she teased.

"A man can always hope," he said, nipping at her bottom lip.

Her hand closed over his manhood, taking it firmly in her grasp. He was hard, and it pleased her to discover how much he wanted her. She wriggled out of her cotton panties, pulled back the covers, and straddled him. She wanted to feel all of him. It had been too long.

"I need you," she whispered in his ear.

Ash growled in response. He placed his hands on her hips as he slid inside her. She closed her eyes, moaning softly. He tried to be gentle, but his need was too great. It felt like the first time – he selfishly took all that she gave, and she urged him on.

When she tilted her head backwards once more, his hands fisted in her hair and his mouth claimed her throat. With his every thrust, she rose with him. Her body begged for release, though she didn't want this moment to end. A scorching heat raced through her as her urgency built.

Ash's eyes burned into hers. She could sense his need was intense. She wanted to scream. To curse. To beg. Instead she whispered his name over and over as he took her higher and higher.

When she reached her climax, this time she screamed out his name. He muffled her cries with his mouth as he found his own release.

"I love you, Roe." He pulled her close, cradling her in his arms. He knew he'd never get enough of her.

Rosalie snuggled up next to him, smiling. "I love you too, Ash." He was all she'd ever wanted; someone she could find herself in and lose herself in at the same time.

The two lay together, soaking up the early hours of the dawn — neither wanting to join the rest of the world. These stolen hours were no one's but theirs.

CHAPTER TWENTY-SIX

With the battle only days away, Ash and Stryker met each night to plan for the big day. With everything they were able to gather from the villages, coupled with what the master of the house bequeathed to them, they felt confident in their stockpile of weapons. But both men worried how their army would stack up against Lord Zebadiah's.

"Okay that's two Inflictors," Ash said, adding to the list on the chalkboard. "But we have to strike the Gifter."

"Jrynton's out?"

Ash nodded. "He's not a fighter. He'll prepare the men as much as possible, but after that … we're on our own."

Stryker rubbed his chin as he inventoried the board. The left side listed the names and powers of the *variants* who agreed to support the Liberation Alliance. The right side listed the names and powers of those Lord Zebadiah had at his disposal – that is if their intel proved accurate.

In many ways, the two sides appeared evenly matched, but there were a few glaring shortfalls.

"I'd hate to say it," Stryker said, "but we could use a Blocker."

Ash laughed, despite his worries. "Should we swing back by Mabel Village? It's a little out of our way."

Stryker snorted. "Getting rid of him didn't seem to clear up Marx's visions any."

Ash nodded in agreement. "I'm sorry, man. How we handled that should have been a joint decision."

"Forget about it. We've all been a little out of sorts lately."

The two men turned back towards the board.

"Looks like we have a couple more Seducers than Lord Zebadiah. That might work in our favor. They could help us sway the enemy," Stryker offered.

"They have a Borrower. Goes by the name of Dekler. That worries me," Ash admitted.

"How so?"

"Because no matter who we bring to the fight – no matter how strong our powers – he can mimic any of them; borrow them for his own."

Stryker nodded. He folded his arms in front of him, puffing out his chest with pride. "We have a Discloser and they don't."

"Worthless power," Ash muttered, winking in Stryker's direction.

"Sure wish we had a Blocker," he shot back.

When Ash arrived at the room late that evening, Rosalie was stepping out of the shower.

"What kept you?" she asked, toweling off her hair then wrapping her body in the towel. These days she'd gotten used to his late arrivals. It didn't upset her. She knew there was important work to be done. But that didn't keep her from missing him. Or from being curious.

"Stryker and I were taking inventory of our assets," he told her honestly.

She laughed. "Exactly what does that mean?"

"We were comparing the powers of those with the Liberation Alliance against the powers Lord Zebadiah's people have."

She was about to ask how he found out what sort of powers Castle Druin might hold but then decided knowing how he obtained the information would probably make her worry more than she already did. Instead, she asked a different question she'd been curious about.

"Does Stryker have a power?"

The question took Ash by surprise. "Why do you ask?"

"You have a power. He's second in command. It would stand to reason he would also have a power."

He kissed her on the chin. "You think too much."

"Does he?"

"He doesn't like people to know about it," Ash admitted.

"Why not?"

"Because he knows it makes people uncomfortable."

"I think all *variants* make people uncomfortable."

"The ignorant people, yes, but his power seems to make most people uncomfortable – even most *variants*."

"Go on?"

"He's a Discloser," Ash said, sensing she wasn't going to let it go.

"I'm not familiar with that one."

"If he touches you, he has the power to disclose your deepest secret."

Rosalie took a step back and tried to recall if Stryker had ever touched her. She remembered he'd patted her arm after she'd saved his brother. She pondered what his power might have unveiled. Then again, it didn't particularly matter. Her secrets didn't run deep.

"You see," Ash spoke up, breaking her train of thought. "You're already weirded out."

She laughed. "I did have a moment of panic. But then I remembered, I'm like an open book."

"Yeah, Stryker already filled me in on that."

"What?" she said, appalled.

"I'm kidding. He only channels his power as a last resort – and rarely reveals to anyone what he discovers. It's a sore spot for him."

"Hmm... Well, since I saved his brother, I'm sure he'll tell me. I wonder what sort of secrets he knows about you."

She shot him a wink and Ash narrowed his eyes. "I'm also an open book," he said. She rolled her eyes in response.

CHAPTER TWENTY-SEVEN

With Ash and his army busy outside with their daily training regimen, Rosalie rolled up her sleeves and got to work inside. The mansion came with a fully staffed kitchen, but she wanted to do something special. The Liberation Alliance had been working tirelessly to prepare for battle – and not all were lucky enough to have their own room with a king-sized bed to rest up in. Most of the soldiers slept in bunk houses towards the back of the property.

"What do you need from us?" the head cook, Arilisa, asked. She had been beyond excited when Rosalie broached the idea of preparing a fancy meal for the entire Liberation Alliance.

Wanting it to be a surprise for everyone, Rosalie didn't let anyone but the household staff in on her plan. She'd thought about telling Othelia and Lexis but decided they had been working just as hard and deserved a treat (though, admittedly, they were amongst the lucky ones to have a bedroom to rest up in). Since they'd arrived at the mansion, her two friends had kept busy grooming horses, mending pelts, and sharpening blades. Lexis even trained with the army on occasion.

Rosalie turned to Arilisa and asked, "Do you have any china?"

"We do. The master of the house used to hold great parties here." Her eyes glistened as she reminisced. "Oh, I miss the sound of this house when it was bursting at the seams with people having a good time."

"Well, let's bring out the china. And what about wine? Not so much where everyone gets carried away, but I thought a few bottles on each table might be nice."

"We should have plenty. That is if Phynley here didn't drink it all." Arilisa winked at a young man on her kitchen staff.

He blushed and grinned good-naturedly. "What can I say? I didn't want good wine to go to waste."

Arilisa shook her head, laughing, then immediately switched into planning mode. "Phynley, if you wouldn't mind getting the wine. Take Kechpin with you. And Mixxun, how about if you and Trappson fetch the china? Bring it to the great dining hall. Bigginsmae, Reshaun, if you two could start wiping down the tables and putting on the linens, Rosalie and I will start on the menu."

With the staff dispersed on their errands, Rosalie and the head cook traded ideas for the feast. "What about daulket with a marmalade sauce?" Arilisa suggested.

Rosalie thought about it. "It does sound delicious. The only problem is we've been eating a lot of daulket meat lately."

"Not with my marmalade sauce."

"True." Rosalie agreed. "We also have quite a bit of tuskentee meat left." She smiled to herself, remembering the pride of bringing down the great beast. "Do you have a special recipe you prepare with that?"

The head cook's face lit up. "I do. I have a mouthwatering recipe that's been in my family for years."

"Perfect. Well, what if we offered both courses? Give them a variety?"

"I think I like you," Arilisa said. She produced two aprons from a drawer and tossed one to Rosalie. "I don't let many folks into my kitchen, but you can join me anytime."

While Arilisa and Rosalie worked away in the kitchen, the rest of the staff filed in and out, asking for their next task. There were napkins to press and fold, goblets to set out, silverware to polish, and additional tables and chairs to be brought in from the outbuildings. Elaborate candlesticks were set on each table.

"This is beautiful," Rosalie mused. She'd slipped out of the kitchen for a break and to check out the great dining hall. Overflow seating spilled into the hallway. It would be a tight fit to host the entire Liberation Alliance, including the new recruits, but Rosalie loved that every person would get to partake in such a special feast.

Arilisa came up beside her and patted her hand. "They're going to love this."

"Thank you for helping make all this possible."

"It is our absolute pleasure."

Rosalie stepped outside to find Ash. She wanted him to make the announcement for everyone to wash up before dinner.

"All of us?" he asked when she broached the subject.

"Yes, all of you."

"Roe, wow, that had to be quite an ordeal to throw together. No wonder you've been avoiding me all day." He clasped her hands in his and stared into her green eyes. "So, does this mean I don't get you all to myself tonight?"

"Hmm…" she teased. "I suppose there's always dessert."

When he leaned in to kiss her, she side-stepped him, giggling. "Wash up. Give the order. Dinner will be ready in precisely thirty minutes."

The look of awe on the faces of the Liberation Alliance when they entered the great dining hall was all the thanks Rosalie and the kitchen staff needed. The head cook had suggested the food be pre-plated and include a portion of both main entrees. She'd offered the recommendation to save time – but it also made the table look beautiful and the delectable aroma of fresh baked bread and basted tuskentee meat wafted in the air. Rosalie was glowing with excitement at seeing the room packed full of people who were obviously enjoying themselves.

"Your men clean up nicely," she commented to Ash over dinner.

"So do you," he said, admiring the short, black dress she wore.

"Oh, this ol' thing," she teased. "Apparently there were some wild parties held here back in the day. The head cook found this dress amongst the *lost and found* and had it cleaned and pressed for me."

"Thank goodness for wild parties," Ash told her. He covered her hand with his and planted a kiss on the side of her head.

Blushing, Rosalie switched topics. "Your men seem to be enjoying the food."

"You've probably spoiled them," he said, pretending to be cross. "Now they'll be demanding meals like this from here on out."

Marx joined the party, seating himself next to Ash and taking everyone by complete surprise. The Discerner typically kept to himself.

"You came," Ash said, stating the obvious.

"I wasn't about to miss this spread."

"Rosalie," Ash said, "I don't believe you've met my old friend Marx."

She tensed, then blushed. "Uh, I don't believe we have," she lied, extending her hand. "I'm Rosalie."

Marx took her hand in his. "It's a real pleasure to meet you," he said, casting a wink in her direction.

"Am I missing something?" Ash asked.

"Nope, just flirting with your girlfriend."

Rosalie pressed her napkin to her lips to stifle a laugh, and her shoulders relaxed. Between bites of food, she concentrated on the faces of her guests. Lexis, who sat across from her, and next to Othelia, was the only person who looked a little melancholy. Rosalie also noticed she'd barely touched her food.

"Everything okay?" she finally asked.

"What's that?"

She spoke up louder, assuming Lexis couldn't hear her over the noise. "You look a little down."

"I'm okay. It's just a bit warm in here." Perhaps she worried her lack of enthusiasm offended Rosalie because she offered a tight smile and added, "But the food is delicious. This was so nice of you."

"I didn't do it alone. The staff here is incredible. I'll introduce you to them later."

Lexis shrugged, noncommittal and went back to picking at her food.

Othelia glanced over at her Rosalie, shrugged, then winked at her. "Can't please everybody," she mouthed, to which Rosalie tried not to snort with laughter.

"Well, I for one am enjoying this," Ash whispered seductively. "But I was sort of more interested in that dessert you mentioned earlier."

Once the meal was over, Rosalie surprised her dinner party with entertainment. The mansion boasted a spacious events room complete with a small stage and a grand piano. According to the staff, the stage had been used by some of the finest musicians and actors. Tonight, what Rosalie had prepared would have to do.

The Liberation Alliance of two hundred plus filled the events room and took their seats. Nervously Rosalie peered through the curtain from behind stage. She had butterflies in her stomach when she spotted Ash and Stryker in the front row. She began to worry she'd overreached assuming all these people would care to hear silly folk songs with a battle looming before them. It had been her hope the music would lift their spirits and get their minds off fighting for a while. But now, seeing the room packed with people, she was having second thoughts.

"It's just stage jitters," a man named Sable whispered beside her. He was the head maintenance man for the house, and to Rosalie's recent discovery, a fine guitar player.

"I sure hope so."

The curtain opened and everyone applauded, though they had no idea what they were about to see. Rosalie stepped forward to the microphone at center stage. She'd changed into a long, shimmering dress Arilisa found for her. It hugged her curves and made her feel sexy and confident. The two musicians she'd managed to wrangle into helping her joined her on stage. Sable stood tall, clutching his guitar. It had always been his dream to perform on that very stage he himself had prepared for so many fine performers in years past. Beside him stood Etheleena, cleaning staff by day and violinist any chance she had. The piano loomed behind them.

"Good evening," Rosalie said once the applause died down. "I know everyone has been working really hard, and to show our appreciation, we've prepared some music for your entertainment."

There was applause and some hoots and hollers from the crowd. Rosalie took a breath and prayed they weren't disappointed.

"Beside me is Sable, on guitar, and Etheleena on the violin."

More applause. Sable glowed with pride and Etheleena took a humble bow.

"And, while I'm told in the past this stage hosted many fine singers, I'm afraid tonight you'll have to put up with me." She flashed a smile, drew courage from the enthusiastic applause, then took a seat at the piano.

As Rosalie's fingers flew across the keyboard, and the first verse of the solemn melody poured from her lips, Ash sat up straighter in his chair. Her voice was smooth and sweet as honey. As she played, there was a genuine sadness to her tune.

When you've gone away,
Please remember me.
I know you can't stay,
But please remember me.

The violin and guitar joined in after the first verse. A hush fell over the crowd as the beautiful music filled the room. Rosalie looked out over her audience, smiling as she belted out the next verse with her powerful, velvety voice.

I've only known you for a little while.
And you always told me you would have to go.
But oh, how I'll miss that tender smile,
There's one thing I'd like you to know.

She leaned in closer to the microphone, her lips almost brushing it as she crooned the sorrowful words. She closed her eyes, shoulders swaying to the music.

I'll never forget your pretty face,
Or the way it felt when you held my hand.
I'll forever miss the warmth of your embrace,
No matter the distance, or what far off land.

So, when you've gone away,
In my heart, you will stay.
I only ask that you remember me.
Ooh, remember me-e-e-e-e.

Rosalie held the last note as the Alliance stood to their feet in applause. She'd managed to transport them away from an approaching battle, and into a great concert hall. Problems were temporarily forgotten as they clapped their hands and eagerly wondered what came next.

She stood, stepped away from the piano, and bowed before her audience. Ash locked eyes with her and watched the adorable way her cheeks turned pink at his gaze.

"If you don't marry her, I will," Stryker said beside him as he clapped his hands together with enthusiasm.

Grinning, Ash said, "Remember you're already married."

He chuckled. "She might make me forget."

"Thank you," Rosalie told the crowd, returning to the microphone at center stage. "Now we're going to speed things up a bit with an old favorite called *Adalinia, Hold My Hand.*"

The familiar song title prompted a huge response from the crowd.

"Oh good, you guys like that one. Okay, well we'll try to do it justice." She nodded to the violin player, who began the quick-paced solo. The crowd stomped their feet to the rhythm, and the guitar player joined in. Rosalie plucked the microphone from its stand. By the time her voice broke in, singing about the sweet-faced Adalinia, she'd captured everyone's hearts.

"Didn't you think Lexis was acting strange tonight?" Rosalie asked when she and Ash were getting ready for bed.

"Maybe a little, but I don't really know her."

She started tossing throw pillows off the bed, then yanked back the covers. "She's usually so friendly. If tonight was the first time meeting her, I would have thought she was…" She trailed off, feeling shame for the unkind words she was about to speak.

Ash began to laugh. "I'm glad to see I'm not the only one who gets under your skin."

"Maybe I'm just being sensitive. I really wanted tonight to be special. She acted like we were… were… putting her out or something." She blew out a breath and threw another pillow. This one bounced off a table leg and rattled a vase perched dangerously close to the table's edge. She shot Ash a sheepish grin. "Oops."

"Everything really did turn out great. Who cares what she thinks? Perhaps being invited to a great feast is an insult in her village." He grinned. "Who knows, maybe where she's from there's a tradition where they boil one of the party guests and serve them for dessert."

She giggled. "Would you stop with talk about dessert? Honestly, is that all you think about?" She grinned at him as she struggled with the zipper of her evening gown.

Ash stared over at her, awestruck. Her gown accentuated her feminine shoulders and narrow waist. She was mouthwatering. When he came up beside her, she turned around, offering him her backside. She scooped up her auburn hair and held it atop her head, giving him full access to the zipper. The dress was cut lower in the back than he'd realized. He shook his head with appreciation, then unzipped it, slowly. When the shimmering gown fell to the floor, he placed a kiss on her bare back, between her shoulder blades. "Well, it is now," he murmured, referring back to her comment about dessert.

The dawn had barely broken when Ash and Rosalie were roused from sleep by a frantic knocking on their bedroom door. As Ash scrambled out of bed and worked to pull on his pants, the knocking became more intense.

"I'm coming," he grumbled. Bleary-eyed, he trudged to the door and yanked it open.

Dillinger stood on the other side of the door. "I'm sorry, sir. Stryker wanted me to tell you that we've had a deserter."

"I don't like that term. We no longer have prisoners, and no one is under any obligation to stay."

"Understood, but this case is a little different. It's the nature of why the person left. Stryker thought it was best if you two met in private to discuss it."

"So why are you here instead of Stryker?" It was unlike Ash to act so cross, but he was still groggy, and Dillinger wasn't making any sense.

"He's already in Marx's room, discussing it with him."

Ash raked his fingers through his hair. "I see. Who is the deserter?"

"Best if Stryker explains everything to you, sir."

"Alright. Tell him I'll be right there."

Dillinger nodded, then made his retreat.

"What's going on?" Rosalie asked. She'd only caught about every third word but had heard enough to understand it wasn't good news.

"I'm not sure yet. I've got to talk to Marx and Stryker. I'm not sure how long I'll be, but I'll come back, okay?"

"Okay," she said, yawning and lying her head back on the pillow.

He gave her hair a tug. "Go back to sleep." He kissed her cheek, then stood to leave.

"Love you," she murmured, already drifting back to sleep.

He stared at her for a moment longer before pulling on his shirt and shoes. He wasn't looking forward to whatever Stryker and Marx had to tell him.

"Let's have it," Ash said, stepping into Marx's room.

"Well, good morning to you too," he said sarcastically.

Ash crossed his arms in front of his chest but didn't say anything.

Marx cleared his throat and stared pointedly at Ash. "We had a deserter last night."

"That part I heard." His tone was impatient.

"It was Lexis."

Ash frowned. "That's surprising. Would explain why she was acting strangely at dinner. And it's a shame to lose a Soother." He narrowed his eyes, arms still crossed. "Not sure if that's worth getting me out of bed this early."

Stryker spoke up. "No, but this is. She left a note." He handed Ash a folded-up slip of paper.

Unfolding it slowly, Ash fought to appear calm. He didn't need bad news this late in the game. He read the contents of the note, crumpled it up, then shoved it in his pants pocket. "You didn't see anything like this coming?" The question was directed at Marx.

"I'm a Discerner not a freaking psychic or miracle worker."

"Relax, I'm not accusing – just asking."

"Why don't you just say what's on your mind? That I'm losing my gift. I can't see what happens to Rosalie. I didn't see this."

"Hey, hey, Marx," Ash said, softening his tone. "No one is saying that."

"Yeah, Marx," Stryker chimed in. "No one is suggesting you held anything back or are losing your gifts. I'm a Discloser, and I got nothing when I met her. We just need to figure out what happened, and what we're going to do about it."

"Sorry," Marx said. "I guess I'm just mad at myself. I thought once Talon was gone things would get clearer. That just hasn't been the case. I blame myself for this one. I really feel like I should have seen it coming."

"Maybe we have another Blocker amongst us and don't know it," Stryker offered. "Maybe *they* don't even know it."

"It's a possibility," Marx said. "But I fear something else is at play. My intel says Lord Zebadiah has gotten deep into sorcery. It's likely he's channeling something that blocks my visions related to him."

Stryker asked, "So, what do we do?"

Ash rubbed his chin, then straightened his shoulders. "We just do our best. And we fight. As planned."

"What did you find out?" Rosalie asked when Ash rejoined her. She was already up, dressed, and pacing the floors.

He sat on the edge of the bed. "Well, you were right about Lexis acting strangely."

She sat down next to him. "Really, what happened?"

"She left us last night."

"Do you know where she went."

"She didn't say."

"Did she say why?

"She did."

"Ash, what did she say?"

He hesitated, thought of glossing over the facts, but decided in favor of full disclosure. He fished the note from his pocket, smoothed it out, and handed it over to Rosalie.

She opened the note and read it aloud.

It is with a heavy heart that I let you know I am leaving the Liberation Alliance. I can no longer live a lie. You see, it wasn't by chance that you found me in Grockdurn. I was planted there by Lord Zebadiah. He knew you would keep me for my soothing powers. I was sent to be a spy amongst your camp. The idea was to sneak out tonight and report back to Castle Druin on your plans. But I've had a change of heart. I've made friends here and I see now that I was on the wrong side. But although I won't be relaying your plans to Lord Zebadiah, I can't stay. If he finds out I betrayed him, he will never let me live. I also know my betrayal of your trust is unforgiveable. Although I can't expect your forgiveness, I hope you won't hate me; especially you, Rosalie and Othelia. I truly considered you my friends.

Lexis

Rosalie pulled the note to her chest. "I can't believe this."

"I'm sorry, Roe. I know you liked her."

She stood and started pacing again. "I feel like such a fool."

"She fooled all of us. Including Marx, and he's a Discerner."

"Yeah, strange he didn't see that coming."

"Well, whatever you do, don't ask him about it. He's a little sensitive about it these days."

She wanted to agree with him about Marx but knew it would reveal too much. "So, what do we do?"

"Not much we can do. She's gone."

"Yeah, but do you believe her when she says she won't reveal your plans to Lord Zebadiah?"

Ash paused to consider. "I do. But even if I don't, there's no time to change our plans now. We'll just need to be cautious."

She nodded. "I should probably start practicing with your men."

Ash stood to his feet. "What? No, Roe, you aren't coming with us." His words came out sharper than he'd intended them to. He'd planned to break the news more gently.

"Why not? Ash, I want to go with you."

"Absolutely not."

She crossed her arms in defiance. "You're forbidding me, is that it?"

His eyes narrowed. "Women don't customarily go into battle," he said lamely.

"Was Lexis going to get to go? I've seen her practicing."

He didn't answer her question. Instead he said, "Can you just accept I have your best interests at heart, and leave it at that?"

"I don't need you to protect me. I can take care of myself."

He tried to soften his tone. "Ordinarily, I would believe you. But in this instance, I'm saying, no, okay?"

Frustration building, Rosalie continued to press. She wanted the truth – the truth Marx already revealed to her, but she wanted to hear it directly from Ash. "*No*? That's it? Just, *no*. No other explanation?"

He took a deep breath and squared his shoulders. "Roe, I can't explain." How could he explain there was a time he was willing to sacrifice her life for his cause? Now it was unthinkable.

She placed her hands on her hips and narrowed her eyes. "Try."

"Because I can't bear the thought of watching you die. Is that good enough?" Tears of desperation crept in the corners of his eyes.

Rosalie took a step backwards. Although Marx had revealed his visions, nothing prepared her for Ash's reaction to them. His anguish and vulnerability were almost palpable. "Go on," she prodded, softening her tone. She knew what Ash was about to tell her was difficult for him. She knew he risked losing her by confessing the real reason he'd taken her from Mabel Village. The truth was she'd forgiven Ash the moment Marx told her.

Ash pressed his fingertips to his forehead, rubbing between his eyes as if he had a headache coming on. "Before we decided to invade Mabel Village," he started, "Marx had a vision about you." He moved towards her, pulling her close. He bent down and rested his forehead on hers, then drew back once more and took another deep breath.

"He saw you," he continued. "Saw your powers. How strong you are…" His eyes burned into hers, silently pleading for her forgiveness. Or for her to ask him to stop.

"Go on," she said instead.

"Through his visions, Marx was convinced that you were crucial to our victory against Druin. Against Lord Zebadiah."

"Then you have to let me…"

"But he also saw you die," Ash blurted out. "Do you hear me? You die. End of story."

"And what happens if I don't go?" She wanted him to reveal the whole truth.

"It's uncertain." He stroked her cheek.

She swatted his hand away. "It's uncertain. Exactly. If you go into battle without me, and something happens to you, do you want me to live with the regret that I could have done something?"

He shot her a sharp look. "His vision changed. Our success is almost eminent."

"It's almost eminent *if* I go," she challenged.

"That part's not clear."

"And it's also not clear if you'll still win if I don't go."

Ash remained silent.

"I can't take the risk," he finally said.

She was about to remind him there was a time he had no qualms about taking such a risk with her life, but she knew her words wouldn't serve any purpose but to hurt him. "You're risking your men," she said instead.

"No. No, I'm not. I'm preparing everyone as much as possible. Not everyone has the luxury of a Discerner. Most people approach a battle without knowing the outcome. We're operating with the *real* information we have. My men are strong. Trained. We will be victorious."

Rosalie wondered who he was trying to convince more – her, or himself. "You'll have a better shot if I'm there."

"I just can't."

"But…"

"Roe, please." His voice cracked and his eyes darkened. "Please give me this one. I can't lose you. It's not even an option I'm willing to consider. If we win, but I lose you – it's not a win."

Sensing she wasn't getting anywhere, she placed a hand on his shoulder. "Okay," she spoke softly.

She was purposely vague, but her response seemed to please him. He slipped his arms around her waist and pulled her closer. A thousand emotions stirred inside him. Relief, for starters. Relief she didn't hate him once she'd learned he'd taken her prisoner knowing it might mean sacrificing her life. Perhaps that part hadn't sunk in yet. Amazement. Amazement that, although she heard the risk, she was still willing to join him on his conquest. And finally, love. Deep love for this beautiful woman, fused with scorching desire. When his lips met hers, there was an urgency there likened to when he'd kissed her for the first time.

Rosalie's hands fisted in his hair. "Make love to me," she whispered.

He pulled back from the kiss. His hands framed her delicate face, his thumbs tracing her full lips. "I love you, Roe."

"I know," she said. "But I still might make you prove it." She began to unbutton her shirt. She stripped off her clothes as she walked backwards toward the bed.

Ash grinned, unbuckling his belt and sliding it from his belt loops. He let it fall to the floor next to her clothes.

He shook his head as he stared back at Rosalie's naked form. Everything inside him longed to be closer to her. "What you do to me," he groaned.

Her body quivered with pleasure as he stripped off the rest of his clothes and fell into bed with her. He made love to her slowly. Perhaps they both knew it might be their last time. Rosalie reveled in his every move, holding back tears of unbridled admiration mingled with unspoken regret.

CHAPTER TWENTY-EIGHT

Lord Zebadiah gazed at Siranya as she approached him. She'd been unable to locate any *variants* in the last several villages they passed through, and he'd begun to suspect she was losing her gift. But she'd done well today. Her Receptor skills were strong, and she'd located four *variants* to add to his collection. Best of all, she'd located another Receptor – a young male of twenty.

Zebadiah was surprised Siranya pointed the Receptor out. She had to know the man posed a threat to her. Then again, perhaps she felt assured in her place. Or perhaps she realized she'd been coming up short and needed to produce.

The evil lord smiled at her. With her red, glossy lips, she smiled warmly back, sidling up beside him and slipping her arm through his. She thought she loved him; he knew. But he also knew it wasn't truly love she harbored for him. She admired his position of power – desired to harness it.

To him, she was expendable. Wicked smart. Wicked beautiful. But her thirst for control was a risk to him. He would keep her around as long as she served his purpose. Then, one day, he'd put his hands around her swan-like neck and watch the life drain out of her pretty face.

"You look so serious," she cooed, interrupting his thoughts. "Something troubling you?"

His eyes twinkled with depraved amusement. "Nah. As long as I have you, no one can touch us."

His words brightened her face. "Where to now?"

"The weather is changing. My collection is strong. Now, we return to Druin."

"Just one more village," she pouted, eyes darkening with bloodlust.

Lord Zebadiah cocked his head to the side and smiled a nefarious smile. He admired her tenacity. "Patience," he said. "There will be another season. Besides, I want to check in on the lab experiments. I'm told we're getting close." His body tingled with excitement.

CHAPTER TWENTY-NINE

When Ash stepped out of the shower and into the bedroom, he expected a fight before his departure for Druin, but Rosalie greeted him with a kiss instead. She stood on her tiptoes and slipped her arms around his neck. He took her in his arms, holding her tight while burying his head in her hair. "I'll be back for you soon," he said.

"Be careful," she whispered back.

He took a step back to study her. Her eyes were red-rimmed and puffy, as if she'd been crying. But her smile was radiant. "I love you more than anything," she told him. She felt raw. Uncertain of their fate.

"Don't say it like we're saying goodbye," he told her. "I love you too, Roe. And everything's going to be okay."

She smiled back at him, but her smile didn't reach her eyes. She couldn't suppress her sadness. "You're going to make a great leader," she told him after a brief silence passed between them.

He thought the statement strange. If she was so certain he would be victorious, why was she so melancholy? He pulled her close and kissed her once more.

She followed him outside. The first leaves of the harvest season had fallen, creating a dazzling blanket of orange and gold. She stood by, trying to be brave as he mounted his horse. "Shyde, you're going to be a beautiful sight to come back to," he told her, and she laughed despite her sorrow. He slapped the reins, then galloped ahead to take the lead amongst his army. When he turned his head to wave goodbye once more, Rosalie wasn't anywhere to be seen.

Castle Druin stood stark and gray in the distance, surrounded by a forest of diseased trees. Ominous clouds blocked out the sun. Stryker and Ash led the way through the dense fog, the Alliance close behind. The horses grew unsteady. It was as if they could sense the evil of such a place.

"Easy, boy," Ash spoke into his horse's ear. He stroked the beast's mane while applying pressure to the reins. The horses weren't the only ones with the jitters. Ash felt self-doubt forming in his belly. He'd done the right thing for Rosalie, forcing her to stay behind. But was it the right thing for his men? What lives had he unknowingly sacrificed by his decision? Perhaps he wasn't the leader he once thought he was.

"It was the right call," Stryker said, riding up beside him.

"What?"

"With Rosalie. I couldn't have that on my conscience either. Marx's vision wasn't clear. And I believe we make our own destiny." He winked in Ash's direction, slapped the horse with the reins, and rode ahead.

"You ready?" Marx whispered to Rosalie from where she lay hidden in the wagon, behind the boxes of ammunition.

Rosalie popped her head up. "Ready," she smiled, looking around. She pulled bits of hay from her hair before she stood to her feet. Her hair was pulled back in a tight braid, making her look younger, somehow.

Marx stared at her, straining to glimpse a vision of how it might all end. Although Rosalie's presence strengthened his vision of victory, he could no longer foresee her fate. "Are you sure about this?" he asked, starting to doubt their plan. He'd grown fond of her too and didn't want to see anything happen to her. He also loved Ash like a son, and he knew if anything happened to Rosalie, Ash would take it hard.

"We've been over this." Her tone was stern, but she smiled back at him. "I'm ready."

"We're going to sneak you around back," he said more self-assuredly.

She knew she projected more confidence than she felt. Inside she was a bundle of nerves. She wasn't sure what made her more anxious – confronting her mortal enemy or facing Ash's wrath once he discovered she'd gone against his wishes and tagged along for the battle. But when presented with the facts, she knew she didn't have much choice. If her presence increased Ash's chances of victory by even a fraction, it was the right thing to do.

Rosalie and Marx slipped out the back of the wagon. They darted for the tree line and hunkered down until the Liberation Alliance was out of their sight line. Slowly, the pair made their way through the cover of trees, circling to the backside of the castle. Rosalie's heart pounded in her chest and her breathing was staggered. Bravery faltering, she began to wonder if she was up for the challenge.

"You're doing great," Marx whispered.

She offered him a tight smile. She squeezed the emerald around her neck, mumbled a small prayer to the gods, and pressed forward.

The shrubbery around the castle was thick and full of thorns. Marx pulled a dark hooded cape from his satchel and offered it to her. She slipped it on, pulling the hood over her head and sliding her braid over her shoulder.

"This is where I leave you," he said with regret. "I need to rejoin the men before they notice I'm gone." He gave her braid a soft tug as his eyes clouded with emotion.

"I'll be fine."

"I know you will," he lied. He wished he knew for certain. He longed for clarity of her future. But no matter how hard he tried, or how long he meditated, his visions were incomplete. This was as far as his visions led him.

Rosalie peered back at him from beneath the dark hood. A soft rain began to fall, and wispy, auburn curls formed on her forehead. This is where her bravery would be put to the test. She pulled Marx into a fierce hug. "I'll be fine," she said again – more for her own benefit.

When Ash and his men neared the castle gate, they were surprised to find it guarded with more men than anticipated. "No matter," Ash said aloud. "Our plans don't change."

The Druin army drew their weapons, ready for a fight. Ash's army followed suit. "Hold steady," Ash warned his men.

When they were close enough, he gave his two Inflictors the signal, and they began a chant which left the army of Druin doubled over and clutching their bellies.

"More," Ash ordered.

The Inflictors chanted louder. The Druin army bellowed and rubbed their eyes as if they were experiencing a chemical burn.

It was now time for the Fabricator to work his magic. He closed his eyes and concentrated on projecting a tranquil setting. Ash's men shut their eyes to block out the spell, but the Druins had not been trained. The Liberation Alliance vanished before their eyes – replaced by a tropical garden with exotic birds and a stream flowing through it. The Druins lowered their weapons and strained their eyes to see clearly; but where a threatening army once stood, there was a welcoming waterfall and a magnificent sunrise.

As planned, Ash dismounted from his horse and approached his disconcerted enemies. He channeled his powers, speaking in firm but hushed tones and bending the men to his will. Most surrendered voluntarily, stepping aside to let Ash and his soldiers through. Some resisted. A Blocker, for one; but Ash's men were prepared. They worked swiftly to restrain the resistance.

Within the castle walls, the soldiers fanned out in search of Lord Zebadiah. Marx sidled up beside Ash and patted him on the back.

"Where have you been?" Ash barked.

"I stayed behind to clear my head; hoping to get a clearer read on the situation," he lied.

"And?"

He shrugged his shoulders. "We'll probably win."

Ash cracked a smile. "Wow, what a confidence booster."

Marx laughed, but his face was etched with worry. Somewhere on the castle grounds, Rosalie was left to defend herself; shouldered with the burden of saving them all.

Rosalie tried to pretend her cloak made her invisible as she clawed her way through the thicket. Arrows whistled through the air and landed several yards away, shaking her confidence and putting her off balance. She paused to take a breath, closing her eyes and willing her courage to return. When she reopened her eyes, she concentrated on her surroundings.

Beyond the brush she could make out two sentries perched on tree stumps, playing a card game. She knew Ash and his men would be approaching the front castle gate and was surprised how inattentive the men seemed to their post. Perhaps it was a trap. No matter. She knew what she needed to do. The man that she loved and the people she'd grown fond of depended on her, even if they were unaware of her presence. She lowered her hood, squared her shoulders, and stepped out of the thicket. With renewed energy and strength, she walked towards the two men.

As predicted, the sentries seized Rosalie and led her straight to Lord Zebadiah who sat smug upon his throne. With his dreadful smile and black robe covering his long, stringy hair, he looked menacing; the embodiment of evil. Rosalie supposed that was the point. Flaming torches and animal skulls lined the aisle leading to his throne. The air was pungent with the smell of rot and smoke and she resisted the urge to hold her nose.

A pretty but fierce-looking woman in a flowing gold gown and gaudy, jewel-crested headdress stood beside Zebadiah. The woman whispered something in his ear, the pair exchanged an impish laugh, then the woman walked down the red, carpeted steps to where Rosalie stood.

Rosalie remained ramrod straight as the woman approached her. The woman lifted a strand of Rosalie's hair and pressed it to her nose, inhaling it. "You have many powers," she observed. Her voice was silky but cold.

"You must be Siranya, the Receptor."

The Receptor smiled. Instead of softening her look, the smile made her appear wicked, and Rosalie shuddered involuntarily.

"Women with powers are rare. And to be a Mender, a Soother, *and* a Healer." She paused and ran a chilling index finger over Rosalie's cheek while making a clucking sound with her elongated tongue. "You would be such an asset to our cause I can almost *taste* it." Siranya's face was inches from Rosalie's. She enunciated *taste* as if the idea of joining forces with Rosalie was bursting off her taste buds.

Taking a step back, Rosalie glared back at Siranya. "I would never join you."

Lord Zebadiah chuckled from his perch. "What choice do you have my dear?"

She glared back at him. His black, beady eyes and gray pallor made her queasy. He beckoned her with his bony index finger. She swallowed the lump in her throat and tried to appear unphased. When she took one step towards him, she felt the pressing of the knife sheathed against her leg and took comfort in knowing it was there.

In a flash Zebadiah was at her side. He jerked her up by the front of her shirt and she sucked in her breath in surprise.

"I suppose there is the one alternative," he said. "Death." His breath was stale, and the word came out as a hiss. Rosalie flinched. At that moment she wished she was the warrior Ash once thought her to be. Then again, he'd only pretended to think it. Her legs wobbled and she fought to control her fear.

"You don't scare me," she lied. "I've heard all about you."

"And just what have you heard?"

"I heard you weren't born with any natural powers of your own."

He glared back at her.

"You're inferior, she continued. "That's why you harbor such a deep hatred for us *variants*. You want to harness our powers while making us suffer."

"I have powers," he countered. He flicked his wrist which sent shockwaves through her. She doubled over in pain, then stood upright again.

Her eyes narrowed in insubordination. "No. What you have is sorcery."

"Sorcery *is* power," he corrected. "Dark magic." He grinned. "I study it. Channel it. Harness it." His eyes gleamed with pride.

"But each season, as you grow more powerful, your heart grows darker. You've dammed yourself. You'll never spend eternity with the gods."

"I *am* a god." Lord Zebadiah was inches from her face. When he slipped his hands beneath her cloak and placed them on her waist, she shuddered and closed her eyes. His hands trailed to her inner thigh where they rested on her knife. He caressed her thigh, then slowly removed the knife from its sheath. Rosalie's stomach twisted in knots. Her face remained impassive, but inside she was panic-stricken and silently screaming at herself to remain calm.

"Nice piece of hardware."

"I find it gets the job done." She lifted her chin in defiance.

Lord Zebadiah's eyes narrowed and one of his men appeared by his side. "Take her to the lab," he ordered. "We'll soon find out how deep her loyalties run."

Despite her terror, those were the words Rosalie had hoped for. It meant things were going according to plan.

The lab looked as intimidating as she'd imagined it would – stark, cold, and sterile. Like most labs there were stainless steel workspaces furnished with vials, pipettes, autoclaves, and other scientific instruments. Massive, wooden fume hoods lined the center aisle. But instead of caged animals bordering the outer walls, there were holding cells full of the *variants* Lord Zebadiah had captured along the way.

When one of Zebadiah's men forced her into a cell, she feigned resistance but was ultimately relieved to be behind bars. It put some distance between her and her enemies. After yelling empty threats at her captors through the bars, she shed her restricting cloak, then turned to face her cellmates.

CHAPTER THIRTY

With the vast size of the Liberation Alliance, it was every man on deck for the people of Druin, forcing the scientists out of the lab and the sentries away from their posts – just as Marx had predicted. It took Rosalie only moments to pick the lock using the file she'd hidden in her underneath clothes. In Zebadiah's arrogance, he hadn't searched her thoroughly. He'd confiscated the knife but hadn't bothered to look further.

The cells in the lab were cramped with people from countless townships, with a myriad of special powers. As she worked to free them all, she realized some might be dangerous criminals who actually needed to be imprisoned, but she didn't have time to worry about that now.

Many of the *variants* fled once she released them. They didn't have an appetite for a fight. The few who remained looked to Rosalie for guidance.

"Search the lab and nearby rooms. Find anything you can use as a weapon," she ordered. "We'll meet back here in ten minutes."

She rummaged through the lab first, hoping to find scientific instruments that could double as weapons. When she reached a cluttered workspace, she stopped short. A black and red lab journal sat, open-faced. She picked it up. There were sketches of the human body, formulas scrawled across the pages, but two bold words caught her eye. MELDED POWER. She blinked twice, trying to make sense of the data. Her brow furrowed in concentration as her eyes skimmed the open pages. "They were designing a serum for a superpower," she said aloud.

One of the newly freed prisoners came up beside her. "Do you think they were successful?"

With growing concern, she flipped through the pages of the journal until she came to the final page. She stared at the page; sucked in a breath. She noted the empty syringe on the counter, read the labeling on the half-empty beaker beside it, and her eyes brimmed with tears. "I'm afraid so," she whispered.

Rosalie shoved the lab journal into her waistband while she searched the remainder of the lab. She found a half-empty canvas bag, poured out its contents, and began to fill it with prospective weapons. A few scalpels and surgical scissors, bollards made of galvanized steel – pathetic compared to the swords and guns she knew Lord Zebadiah's men carried. She looked around, then hid the journal at the bottom of the bag.

Convinced she'd uncovered all there was to find in the lab, she slung the canvas bag over her shoulder and set off to search the nearby rooms. She was rifling through one of the bedroom dressers when she heard someone approaching from behind. She froze, the hairs on the back of her neck prickling. With painstaking care, she curled her fingers around the closest thing to a weapon she could find. She spun around to meet her aggressor, wielding a brass candlestick.

The man before her held a knife in his hand. Rosalie widened her stance, ready to swing the brass weapon with all her might if the man tried to harm her. But he didn't attack. Instead, he took a step backward and offered a disarming grin.

"Remember me? We just met in the lab?"

Rosalie thought for a moment. She hesitated, then nodded, finally recognizing him as the man beside her when she'd discovered the lab journal; but she didn't lower the candlestick.

"Here, take this," he said, offering her the knife. "I think you'll find it makes a better weapon."

She dropped the candlestick, which hit the floor with a resounding clunk. She eagerly accepted the knife and held it close. It wasn't the knife she was used to carrying, but it would have to do. She secured it in the sheath and felt her confidence return.

"I'm Kipser." He extended his hand. "I'm an Inflictor."

"Rosalie." She shook his warm hand, impressed by his firm grip. "I'm a Healer."

"And a Mender, and a Soother. So I've heard."

"Really?" She felt flattered and a little embarrassed.

He chuckled.

"Thank you for the knife. But what will you use?"

"I've got something a bit better." He pointed to a gun tucked in the waistband of his pants.

The pair circled back to the lab. "I see we've lost a few more," Rosalie mumbled aloud, taking note of the dwindling group of newly released *variants*. She tossed the canvas bag on the floor in front of her. "If you still don't have a weapon, please take what you need," she spoke up.

When the bag was empty, and the modest-sized group of ex-prisoners were as armed as they were able, she continued to give orders.

"Let's spread out. No less than groups of two. Our primary target is Lord Zebadiah. Take note there are friendlies amongst us. The Liberation Alliance is here to help us. Be sure to identify yourselves if needed and be careful out there."

The new recruits nodded in response.

"Good. Then let's move out."

The small group dispersed, but Kipser stayed behind. "I'm going with you," he told Rosalie.

"I'm going too," another man spoke up from the doorway, joining the pair. "I'm Gluge. I'm a Discloser," he said, sticking out his hand.

Rosalie and Kipser nodded, politely introduced themselves, but forewent the handshakes.

Gluge grinned knowingly. It was the typical response he received once he revealed his power. "Before I so readily volunteer," he said, "I guess I should ask. Where are we going?"

"I see you missed the speech," Kipser told him.

Grinning, Rosalie said, "To find Lord Zebadiah and that psycho, Siranya."

"What do we do when we find them?"

"We kill them," she said without hesitation.

CHAPTER THIRTY-ONE

Ash and Stryker remained out front of their men as they crept through the castle hallways in search of the evil lord. The Alliance did their best to keep casualties to a minimum – relying on their powers over their weapons to incapacitate the Druins. The Druin army was not as honorable. They were prepared to fight, and they used both power and weaponry to slay anyone who stood in the way; even their own people.

Swords clashed and guns blazed. The Druin army was vast in numbers, but most were no match for the skilled fighters and honed powers of the Liberation Alliance. In Lord Zebadiah's quest to conquer and harness *variants*, he'd failed to teach and cultivate his own army. Ash reckoned Zebadiah's selfishness would be his downfall.

Rounding the corner of a winding corridor, Ash and his men came face-to-face with a being they weren't prepared for. The man was a beast: standing over seven feet tall with legs like tree trunks and a head like an ox. He wore heavy armor, complete with a brass plated shield and breastplate, and carried a gigantic, silver-tipped axe. The axe would have been difficult for a normal-sized man to lift, but the mountain of a man carried it with ease. He had an aura about him, a visible purple haze that radiated from his skin and darkened his already terrifying features.

"I've been waiting for you," the man spoke. "You might say I was designed for this moment." His eyes gleamed with satisfaction and disdain as he rotated the axe between his grasp.

Ash blinked in confusion. "We're not here for you. We've come to apprehend Lord Zebadiah."

"Well then, allow me to introduce myself. I'm Broagen. And I'm here to make sure that doesn't happen." He lifted the axe. His dreadful words rang out like a chilling melody, low and smooth.

The Liberation Alliance trained their weapons.

Broagen closed his eyes, hissed one undiscernible word, and the weapons of the Alliance fell to the ground. Clangs of metal and a single gunshot from a dropped gun added to the chaos.

"Take it easy," Ash barked at his men before hysteria could set in.

The men scrambled for their weapons, but another mumbled word from Broagen and they were clutching their bellies and screaming out in pain.

Ash squared his shoulders through the pain and faced the man head on. He turned his index finger in a circular motion as he spoke slowly. "You don't want to do this. You can trust us. Let us pass."

The giant of a man laughed at him. "You think your Seducer charms will work on me? I am immune to such antics."

Out of the corner of his eye, Ash saw Stryker and two of his men edging along the sidewall. He sensed they were hoping to sneak up behind the man and defeat him with the element of surprise.

"So, you're a Blocker," Ash said, keeping the man distracted.

The man puffed out his enormous chest. He lifted his axe, then pounded the handle on the floor with a resounding thud. "I have more powers than anyone on Orthron."

"That sounds a bit exaggerated. Show me." Ash knew it was dangerous to toy with the beast, but the distraction was working. Stryker and his men were closing in.

Broagen accepted the challenge. He snapped his fingers and the room morphed into a field of bones. A river of blood flowed through the field. Children stumbled through the bones, crying out for comfort. The ceiling opened up, and droplets of blood poured down on the men.

The sounds of grown men crying out in horror echoed through the room.

"Close your eyes," Ash bellowed out the order. "It's not real."

Another snap of his fingers, and Broagen brought the soldiers to their knees. The men were in agony – a mixture of pain and unexplained grief surged through them. Ash sank to his knees, but kept his eyes trained on his enemy. "That's all you got?" he challenged through his pain.

The man dropped the axe, then clapped his hands together. When he did, a fireball blasted from his fingertips. It shot above the Liberation Alliance, leaving a scorched mark in the wall behind them.

"I missed on purpose," he said wickedly. "The next one…"

Before he could finish his thought, Stryker and the two men with him pounced from behind. Two took Broagen out at the knees. When he sank to the ground, the third jumped on his back and slipped a thin wire around his neck. Broagen flailed, clawing at his neck and screaming in pain and surprise.

"Now," Ash screamed. The Liberation Alliance picked up their weapons and rushed their enemy. The brute tried to defend himself, conjuring up terrifying visions and paralyzing spells, but his powers were weakening as the life drained out of him. The visions were like a mist, the spells no more than a nuisance, and the Liberation Alliance pressed through them.

As a multitude of swords plunged into him, the beastly man cried out in anguish, then crashed to the ground, defeated. Stryker finished him off with a single gunshot to the temple.

"It was him or us," Stryker told the younger men who appeared shell-shocked by the violence. They nodded, but there was a reverent silence for the man's passing.

"I've never seen anyone with that many powers," Marx spoke up, leaning over the fallen man. "I started to fear my visions of our victory had been wrong."

"He was created that way," a man spoke up from behind them.

Ash's men drew their swords, put off by the stranger's presence.

"I mean no harm," the man said, raising his hands in surrender. "I'm only a servant here. Most people of Druin were too terrified to stand up to Lord Zebadiah. Anyone who defied him paid dearly. We've spent years living in fear for ourselves and our families."

"Can you show us where he's hiding?" Ash asked.

"Oh, he's not hiding. He's waiting for you." The man looked down in shame. "He's been preparing for this day."

"Show us."

The Druin servant led the Liberation Alliance through several winding corridors until they reached a grand room. The soldiers inched towards the center of the room. There were archways leading to more corridors and the servant started to look uneasy.

Ash gave the man a sideways look. "Draw your weapons," he bellowed. "He's led us into a trap."

The Druin army flanked them from all sides. The servant slinked away, cowering behind Zebadiah's loyal men.

Ash fought to keep his men calm. "Don't forget your powers," he instructed.

The Fabricator gave Ash a knowing look, then concentrated hard on his surroundings. This time he projected an empty room in place of where he and the rest of the Alliance were standing. The Druin army paused, confused. Next he conjured up a beautiful woman standing in the center. She wore a pink, flowing dress. The dress was sheer, exposing her ample bosoms beneath the fabric, and the Druins stared in awe.

Once the evil army was distracted, Marx knew the time had come to subdue them. "Now," he called out. The remainder of the Liberation Alliance spilled out of the neighboring corridors, surrounding the Druins. Marx had foreseen the ambush, and he had men ready to counter the attack.

When the Fabricator's vision dissolved, the Druin army found themselves surrounded on all sides.

Ash and Stryker grinned at each other, both in on the plan from the beginning.

"You could foresee this, but you couldn't see that powerful freak we just defeated?" Stryker teased Marx.

"I'm pretty sure he was also a Blocker."

"A long-distance Blocker?" Stryker mused, grinning.

"Shut your trap and help me fight," Marx said, motioning to the Druin army who, despite being in a state of shock, were still heavily armed.

"I think you and I both know we've got this one in the bag."

CHAPTER THIRTY-TWO

Rosalie and her new comrades combed the castle for Lord Zebadiah, searching bedrooms, common areas, and dimly lit corridors. They figured they were getting close when they heard battle cries echoing down the hallways. They found the evil lord waiting for them in the atrium of the east wing. He was guarded by a dozen men, all heavily armed.

Gluge drew his sword, Kipser his gun, and Rosalie her knife. Lord Zebadiah threw his head back and laughed. "Is this what you brought to bring me down? Paupers' weapons?"

"*Misery's sting*," Kipser shrieked, conjuring up his Inflictor powers as he thrust out his free hand in anger. All but one of Zebadiah's guards screamed out in agony. The remaining guard and the evil lord smirked in response, unphased.

"That last guard's a Blocker," Rosalie explained, shouting over the screams of distress.

The Blocker closed his eyes in concentration, and before long the screaming ceased.

Kipser thrust out his hand again. His enemies didn't react. His brow furrowed in concentration and confusion.

"He's blocking for all of them now," Rosalie said. "We're going to have to fight the old-fashioned way." She gripped the knife in her hand and rushed forward, Gluge and Kipser close behind her.

The trio put up a noble fight, and managed to pick off a few of the guards, but it was a losing battle. Their only saving grace was that Zebadiah wanted them alive. They soon found themselves cornered; weapons of their enemies trained at their throats.

"Return them to their cells," Zebadiah ordered. "But keep them separated. We don't want to risk…"

"Wait," Rosalie interrupted. "I'll join you."

Lord Zebadiah held up his hand, signaling his guards to hold back. "Join me?"

"Yes, but only if you let my friends go."

Zebadiah made a sound that resembled a laugh, but it sent shivers down her spine. "You think pretty highly of yourself, don't you? Why would I give up two mutants to keep one?"

She squared her shoulders and folded her arms in front of her chest. "Siranya said it herself, how rare I am – having three powers. Think of what you could accomplish if you had full access to them." She spoke the words with confidence, but bile rose up in her throat at the thought of being part of his collection.

"And I'm just supposed to trust that you'll join me without argument?" As the evil lord spoke, he continued to circle her and her comrades, moving in closer each time.

"I guess that's a risk you're going to have to take."

"Or," he said wickedly, "I can imprison all three of you now and then I don't have to sacrifice anything."

"Oh, but you *would* be sacrificing," Rosalie told him. She lowered her voice, forcing Zebadiah to move in closer. The guards stepped back, lowering their weapons and giving their leader room. "I'm offering to *join* you. Meaning I would freely offer my powers to your great army. You could still use some of my blood for experiments if you'd like, but my powers would also be at your disposal."

Intrigued by the prospect of adding Rosalie to his collection, Zebadiah now stood merely inches from her face. He licked his lips in anticipation, his acrid breath coming out in short, excited bursts. Rosalie lifted her left hand and placed it on his shoulder. She spoke a soft chant, letting him feel the warmth of her powers. His eyes closed with pleasure – and that's when she seized her opportunity. With her right hand she retrieved the knife and plunged it into his abdomen.

Zebadiah's eyes went wide with horror and he let out a sickening groan. Rosalie used more force, pushing the knife in deeper. She shuddered at the sound of the knife penetrating his organs. Lord Zebadiah stumbled backwards in surprise.

Too stunned to move, Rosalie sucked in her breath and kept her gaze fixated on him. She'd killed and skinned countless animals with her knife. But she'd never stabbed a person before. It felt different; the way the blade sunk through the flesh. The feel of warm, thick blood on her hands.

The evil lord cursed and spit, spewing blood from his wretched mouth. He pawed at the knife, to no avail, as his eyes darted around the room for someone to help him – but help didn't come. Rosalie watched in horror and relief as the light drained out of his eyes. With one final, terrifying groan, he fell to the floor, dead, her knife buried in his belly.

At seeing their leader fall, the guards fled in terror, but not before one got off a clean shot. The bullet caught Gluge in the temple, killing him instantly. Rosalie was about to rush to his side when she heard a loud, high-pitched shriek, followed by a gunshot. She looked up to see Siranya in the far corner of the room holding something in her right hand. Then a second shot rang out, and Siranya fell. Her headdress crashed to the floor beside her.

Rosalie heard a ringing in her ears as she shuffled in the direction that she'd heard the battle cries. She knew Ash would be there, in the room just beyond the corridor. She felt strange. Disoriented. Warm blood seeped down her clothes. She touched it with her hands; wondered how Zebadiah could have gotten so much on her. The blood pained her. Cursed blood, she reasoned through the fog in her head.

Kipser came to her side. He was shouting something, though she couldn't make it out through the ringing noise that echoed in her head. She noticed the gun in his hand – surmised he must have shot Siranya. *But where did the first shot come from?* It didn't matter. She reached the end of the corridor and entered the great room; saw Ash standing next to Stryker. Both were unharmed. Everything was going to be okay.

CHAPTER THIRTY-THREE

Victory was certain now. Most of the Druin army had fled or surrendered, and the excited shouts from Ash's soldiers, proclaiming Lord Zebadiah had been slain, echoed down the corridors. He thought to himself he'd need to find the man who killed the evil lord and reward him accordingly. He turned to high-five Stryker when he noticed his friend's triumphant expression change to one of confusion and horror.

"Ash?" Rosalie's voice came out in a whisper behind him. He whirled around, surprised to see her. His eyes darted to hers, ready to reprimand her for disobeying his wishes – then his gaze traveled to her midsection. Her hands were pressed firmly to her belly and blood seeped out beneath them. Before he could reach her, she sank to the cold floor.

When he knelt beside her, Rosalie's lips were colorless. Blood soaked her clothing and pooled on the marble floor. She pointed to her pants pocket, desperate to get his attention. By the time he retrieved the piece of paper from her pocket, she'd slipped into a state of unconsciousness.

"Rosalie. Baby, no," he called out to her. "Stay with me." Paper crushed in his grasp, he turned to Marx in anger. "This was your doing, wasn't it? Dammit, I told you she wasn't to be part of this battle." He shook with rage and heartache.

"And I tried to tell you that I believed our victory depended on it."

"You knew she might die."

"She knew the risks. She knew it, and she chose to come."

Ignoring him, Ash slipped his arms under Rosalie's limp body and picked her up. He let the tears fall – for the first time since he could remember.

"She's the one who killed Zebadiah," Kipser offered, still standing in the corridor.

"You see. She saved us all," Marx said, defending her choice. Defending his choice.

"Yeah?" Ash challenged in disgust. "Now who's going to save her?"

CHAPTER THIRTY-FOUR

"**F**etch a doctor," Ash yelled over his shoulder at the closest soldier. He carried Rosalie to the nearest bedroom within the castle walls. Stryker filed in reverently behind him, along with two faithful soldiers. Marx remained in the hallway with Kipser. He was deeply invested in Rosalie's recovery but knew Ash didn't want to see him.

Ash laid Rosalie gently on the bed and knelt beside her. He balled up a blanket and used it as a compress for her wound. When the doctor arrived, Rosalie hadn't regained consciousness and both the makeshift compress and bedsheets were soaked with her blood. A hush fell over the room as the doctor leaned over her, examining her sleeping form. When he raised his head again, he shook his head. "I'm sorry," he murmured, looking at Ash.

"No." The single word came out like a low moan from a wounded animal.

"I can give her something to keep her comfortable until she passes."

"No. You're wrong. Get out," Ash bellowed. He shoved the doctor towards the door. "Find me the Druin detainee they call Dekler," he ordered to the soldier nearest him. When the man hesitated, he shouted, "Now."

The man bolted for the door. The doctor wandered out after him.

Stryker wanted to reprimand his friend – to tell him to calm down. "We'll round up any resistors and assess the injured," he said instead. When Ash didn't respond, he looked at the remaining soldier and jerked his head in the direction of the door. The two men filed out.

Ash kissed Rosalie's forehead and pleaded for her to wake up. She stirred but didn't open her eyes. He cursed himself for allowing Jrynton, the Gifter, to stay behind at the mansion. The man wasn't a fighter, but his ability to help people amplify their powers would be an asset at this moment.

A man entered the room and paused by the doorway. He stood tall with pride, despite being shackled. "You asked to see me?"

"Are you Dekler?"

"I am." The man approached the bed.

Ash took out a key from his shirt pocket and unshackled the man. "Save her," he ordered.

"I'm not a Healer." The prisoner rubbed his wrists as he studied Rosalie's condition.

Ash looked at the man sharply. "But you're a Borrower. You can take on anyone's powers. She's a Healer," he said, jerking his thumb towards the bed where Rosalie lay unconscious.

"By taking on people's powers, I drain them. It'll weaken her. I might do her more harm than good."

"She's going to die if we don't try something."

The man looked hesitant.

"Please," Ash spoke quietly. "Please, you have to save her." His plea was desperate. His eyes glistened with tears and he didn't bother to wipe them away. He didn't care if he looked weak. Rosalie was both his strength and his weakness; he'd come to terms with that. What he couldn't come to terms with was the idea of losing her. He knew he'd be wrecked without her.

The man placed a firm hand on Ash's shoulder. "I will try."

The Borrower crouched down and took Rosalie's frail hand in his. He spoke a string of words Ash couldn't comprehend, then placed both hands on her neck. He slid his hands down her body until they rested on her wounded abdomen. He felt an intense burn and knew the injury was critical.

"She's also a Soother," Ash said, clenching his fists as he paced back and forth. "So, if there's any way you can do this so she doesn't feel pain."

"I'll do my best," Dekler said, not looking up. But he'd had some experience borrowing the power of a Healer. She was going to feel pain – and a lot of it.

Dekler returned his attention to the beautiful woman stretched out before him. He had a feeling it wasn't just his patient's life that depended on his success. He worried about his own fate if he didn't succeed. He'd seen the desperation in Ash's eyes. He hummed and chanted every spell he could recall. His hands and arms burned, an almost intolerable pain, but he continued to work.

Rosalie's body arched and writhed beneath his touch. She screamed out in her sleep and it was all Dekler could do not to scream too.

"You're hurting her," Ash yelled.

"You need to get out of here and let me work."

Dekler howled in pain as the healing process began. He tried a soothing chant to alleviate some of Rosalie's pain, but realized he needed to focus all his energies on channeling her healing powers. Rosalie's lips parted and she shrieked again in agony.

"Stop this," Ash shouted.

"Get out of here and let me do my job," Dekler screamed back. "It's you who might be killing her if you don't let me concentrate."

Ash stared down in reluctance at Rosalie, then left the room, lost for what to do and feeling helpless.

In the hallway, he remembered the piece of paper in his clenched fist. He unfolded it, dreading what he might find. He'd grown tired of notes that contained bad news.

My darling Ash,

I love you more than life itself. I hope you realize this and will come to forgive me in time. Please understand that just as you thought you had to protect me, I had to protect you and do what I thought was best for the cause. If you're reading this, it means I didn't make it, just as you and Marx

feared. But I also hope it means that the battle was won –
and victory is yours. You will go on to be a great leader. In
time, your heart will mend, and you will find love again.
You're stronger than you know. You have my whole heart
and I hope you know that you made me happier than I ever
dreamed possible. My only regret is that I didn't have more
time with you.

Always,
Your Roe

More gut-wrenching than the contents of the letter were the tearstains he saw sprinkled amongst her scrawled words. He caressed the letter with his fingertips. He knew it must have broken her heart to write it. He imagined the sorrow she felt, the devastation, and his tears joined hers on the page. It made sense now – how melancholy she'd seemed before he'd left for battle. He'd misinterpreted it as worry for him. Now he knew what she'd known – that it was *she* who might not return.

He sunk to the floor and pulled his knees to his chest. He did his best, but he couldn't block out the escalating screams coming from the room behind him. Sometimes they were Rosalie's, sometimes Dekler's – sometimes the high-pitched wails didn't sound human. He punched the marble floor in disgust. Pain traveled through his veins like fire as it occurred to him that he may have broken his hand, but he welcomed the distraction. He focused on the pain and tried to block out the cries that penetrated the walls and echoed down the corridor.

The chanting and screams grew to a crescendo. Ash closed his eyes and covered his ears with his hands, but the noise was deafening. And then. Silence.

Ash couldn't move. He felt glued in place; weighted down with grief and anguish. He knew she was dead. Tears streaked down his burly face as he tried to imagine his life from this point forward without Rosalie in it. He'd promised her he'd never let anyone hurt her. He'd unintentionally lied. He'd failed her.

When he stood to his feet, Stryker started to approach him, but he waived him off. He would need to see Rosalie alone to say goodbye. When he turned towards the bedroom, Dekler came through the door, clutching his blood-soaked, scalded hands to his chest. He looked drained as he made eye contact with Ash.

"Is she...?" Ash asked, fearing he already knew the answer.

"She's resting."

The words took a moment to process. "Resting? You mean she's... she's alive?" The hope he hadn't dared to feel flooded through him.

"She's not out of the woods yet, but I think she'll make it."

Ash let out a victory whoop. Despite his throbbing hand, he lifted Dekler off the ground and hugged him. Then he sat him back down, feeling awkward. "I really can't thank you enough."

"She must be someone special," he said, observing Ash's tear-streaked face.

"She's everything to me," he admitted, unashamed.

While Rosalie remained unconscious, Dekler routinely performed healing rituals. During the first day Ash refused to leave her side, despite Stryker's unsuccessful attempts to tear him away.

By day two, Stryker refused to take *no* for an answer. "Look, we all care about Rosalie," he admitted, "but we care about you too. And now that we've conquered Druin, the people need a new leader."

"You can be that leader," Ash said. "You know Roe always thought you were first in command anyway. Maybe she knew you were a better fit."

"That's donkey-shyde and you know it. They need you. Besides, I have a wife and child I'd like to get back home to. You need to pull it together, Ash."

Ash tried to ignore him, but Stryker jerked him up by the shirt collar. "Listen here, you nearly lost her, and it almost destroyed you. I get it. But there are others out there who did lose someone. You owe them your presence."

"I don't owe anybody anything."

"That's not true and you know it. Every one of your men would die for you. Two days ago, they proved that." He let go of Ash's shirt collar and took a step back, softening his tone. "The Liberation Alliance took some hits. And more than that, the people here at Castle Druin lost loved ones too. Everyone is doing the best they can to coexist, but it won't work without someone to lead them. We need to project a united front. The people need a strong leader. They also need to know it's okay to mourn. Now stop being so selfish and get out there and address everyone."

Dekler circled around the bed and stood in front of Ash, placing a firm hand on his shoulder. "I'll take good care of her," he promised.

Nodding, Ash turned to Stryker. "You're right. I just need about five minutes."

When Ash emerged from the room, his injured hand was wrapped in a tight bandage, and he still looked pale and a bit disheveled, but he'd put on clean clothes and combed the hair out of his eyes.

"You're looking … well," Stryker said.

"Liar." Despite his misery, Ash offered a feeble smile.

"Okay, you look like death, now let's get this over with."

Ash called an emergency meeting of the Liberation Alliance. He took inventory of his men. Casualties and injuries were few, but they weren't without impact. Six dead. Fifteen injured. One of the prisoners rescued from Druin was a Mender and had been offering his services around the clock. A Healer would have been better, but unfortunately Rosalie was the only Healer around (or the only one willing to come forward – and Marx was in no condition to try and weed one out).

After speaking with his men, Ash called a mandatory meeting in the auditorium to address the people of Castle Druin. When he took the stage, he did his best to speak calmly, but authoritatively. As he spoke, emotions ran high and varied amongst the crowd. Most were grateful to have someone to look to as a leader, but not everyone was pleased.

Some blamed Ash for the recent loss of a loved one and made their sentiments known. Murmurings from the crowd indicated others feared how their lives might change under his rule. Ash did his best to alleviate their fears, but he knew their acceptance of him and his men wouldn't happen overnight.

Finally, Ash held a private meeting with Stryker. "I need to be with Rosalie until she wakes up," he explained. "I know it probably means I'm failing as a leader, and for that I'm sorry. Declare a week of mourning. Give the people time to bury and grieve for their dead."

Stryker nodded. He knew it was pointless to argue.

"And one more thing," Ash said, turning back to Stryker. "Somebody send for Talon. Rosalie will want to see him when she wakes up."

Three days passed and Rosalie still hadn't regained consciousness. Each morning Ash ordered krisha tea brought up to the room and placed on the table beside the bed. He hoped the aroma of the tea would entice her to wake up. On the morning of the fourth day, as the tea was being set on the table, Rosalie stirred.

When her eyes fluttered opened, she was met with waves of nausea and discomfort. A terrible pain radiated from her stomach – a combination of sharp hunger and an aching, throbbing sensation she'd never felt before. But when her eyes adjusted to the room, and Ash came into focus, her physical ailments were nothing compared to the blow of seeing his unkempt appearance. It was evident he hadn't slept or shaved in days.

"What happened to you?" she whispered. Her throat was dry and her lips felt cracked.

Ash squeezed her hand and leaned in close. "Roe, you're awake."

"And you're a mess," she observed.

He smiled, despite himself. He wanted to lecture her on going into battle when he'd forbade it. He wanted to remind her that her blatant disregard for her own safety led them to this moment. But mostly he wanted to hold her and never let go.

"Did we win?" she asked. She couldn't recall anything past the moment she'd stabbed Lord Zebadiah. Pain racked her body and she tensed, squeezing her eyes shut to block out the hurt.

"We did now," he said. He kissed her and squeezed her hand, ignoring the pain that shot up his wrist. "Can I get you anything?"

She opened her eyes again and gave him a stern look. "Yes," she said, her voice firm. "You can shower and shave. You can pull yourself together and go address your people. They need you now more than ever." Stryker's words echoed in Ash's head and he wondered how much Rosalie overheard while she slept.

He looked down at her, not wanting to leave her side.

"I'll be fine," she assured him. "Now go."

Ash slowly withdrew from her side. He grabbed a quick shower, then shaved. When he emerged from the bathroom, he felt like a new man. He put on fresh clothes before studying himself in the mirror. There were dark circles under his eyes, and it was evident he'd lost a couple pounds, but overall, he looked presentable. He kissed Rosalie once more before she ordered him out. She was feisty for someone who'd been on death's door just a short time ago.

Stryker was relieved to see his friend. "You're looking ... better than expected," he observed.

Ash smiled for the first time in days. "Rosalie's awake."

"Thank the gods."

"Yeah, she gave me a tongue lashing for the way I've been moping about," he admitted.

"Thatta girl. Now what do you say you and I go address the people and attempt to restore some semblance of order to this place?" He slapped his old friend on the back as they made their way to the main courtyard.

"Round up the people," Ash barked to his men. "We have some announcements."

CHAPTER THIRTY-FIVE

With Ash away, Rosalie rose from the bed. She didn't want him to see her in her disheveled condition anymore. She found it difficult to sit up, but she wanted nothing more than a long, hot shower. Nausea nearly knocked her back when she stood to her feet and she realized she'd need to ask for help.

She crept to the door and asked the guard on the other side of the door if he could find Othelia.

"I'd be happy to," he said. "And may I say, we're so happy that you're awake. What you did was very brave. There are many of us who will forever be in your debt."

Rosalie blushed. *Not bad for a huntress*, she thought.

Othelia was over the moons at seeing her friend again. She helped her shower, taking special care of the area Rosalie had been shot, but amazed how quickly the gunshot wound was healing. It looked more like a recent scar than a fresh injury.

"I have been so worried about you," Othelia admitted. "But Ash wouldn't let anyone see you. He holed up here…"

Rosalie smiled at her friend. "I'm sorry I worried everyone."

"Worried doesn't begin to describe what we all felt," her friend confided. "Poor Marx. He's been beside himself since it happened."

A twinge of guilt pulsed through her. "I worried about that. It really was my idea. Marx didn't talk me into it. He only presented the facts."

Othelia snorted. "Try telling that to Ash. Actually, try telling that to Marx."

"I'd like to speak with him."

"Ash is preparing to address the Druins."

"No, not Ash. There will be plenty of time for that later. I meant Marx."

When Marx entered the room, his head was bowed. He looked humbled and drained. To Rosalie's surprise, he'd visibly aged.

"Marx," she said brightly. She was dressed in a white, flowing gown Othelia had found in the closet. Cheeks pink with color, and auburn hair curled loosely down her back and around her shoulders, she looked fresh and elegant. Marx sighed with relief at her appearance.

"Rosalie, I'm so sorry that I talked you into…"

"Stop," she told him. "Don't let your guilty conscience skew the facts. It was my choice. And I'm fine, really."

He embraced her, then stepped back to study her. "You certainly look much better than you did a few days ago."

"Well, I hope so, I'm wearing this fabulous new dress after all," she teased, performing a half twirl.

Marx broke down, burying his head in his hands. "I couldn't see it. I don't know why. I couldn't tell if you'd make it. Shyde, Roe, I couldn't be sure, and I sent you into battle anyways."

"I knew the risk," she interrupted. "Now I don't want to hear any more about it."

"I'm not sure Ash is ready to let it go," Marx grumbled, looking miserable. His old friend hadn't spoken to him since it happened. Guilt and loneliness had plagued him since her injury.

Rosalie smiled kindly. "He worries too much. I'll talk to him," she offered. "Now I brought you here to talk about something else."

Marx perked up. "What's that?" he asked, wiping his eyes with the back of his hands.

She'd made up that last part of course. She hadn't had any reasons for calling on him other than to make sure he was handling things okay. "I need your visions to tell me what outfit will catch Ash's eye," she offered lamely.

Ash was deep into his speech when Rosalie sauntered up beside him and took him by his bandaged hand. She could feel the injury he tried to downplay and she made a mental note to heal his hand while he slept. She knew he wouldn't accept an offer to heal it if she asked him; he was too worried about her own health.

At her presence, the people below cheered. Over the past several days, rumors of how she'd brought down Lord Zebadiah and turned the momentum of the battle had spread through the Liberation Alliance like wildfire. Much of the stories were exaggerated, but all the same the soldiers had a newfound respect and admiration for the attractive, auburn-haired young woman who stood before them.

It wasn't only the Liberation Alliance who took notice of her presence and were thankful for her contributions. Most of Druin lived in fear of their recently departed leader and were beyond relieved to have been liberated from him. Those loyal to Lord Zebadiah were imprisoned in the very cells that once housed the *variants*. A fair deal in most people's eyes.

Ash looked down at Rosalie and smiled. While he waited for the cheering to subside, he bent down and kissed her cheek, fueling the excitement rather than calming it.

Once the crowd quieted down, Ash continued with his address. "We will not abandon this fine city. We will restore it to the great place it was before Lord Zebadiah forcefully took it over. With your help, we will make it grander and more prosperous than it ever was." There was an eruption of applause, followed by a polite silence as the people waited for more.

CHAPTER THIRTY-SIX

Ash had grand plans for restoring Castle Druin, and other than the imprisoned resistors, no one was exempt from the hard labor his plans entailed. While others harvested the crops planted in the early spring, Rosalie found her purpose planting rows of cool season crops to be harvested the following spring. Onions, garlic, peas – even blueberries. It pleased her to be able to use, and pass on, her planting skills. Though she'd never be as skilled as her parents, she felt confident applying all she'd learned would produce a good crop. She'd hoped Othelia could join her, but Othelia's culinary and horsemanship talents meant she was often needed elsewhere.

While she was examining the neat, cultivated rows of seedlings, an elderly woman approached her and extended her feeble hand towards her. When one of the sentries stepped in to try and stop the woman, Rosalie waved him off.

"It's okay." It was important to Rosalie that she forge a strong bond with the people of Druin. She smiled at the woman and shook her hand. "It's wonderful to meet you. What can I do for you?"

The woman's eyes narrowed, and she tightened her grip on Rosalie's hand. "You can go away and leave us alone," she hissed.

Rosalie wasn't sure if it was her imagination, but it looked like the woman's eyes turned black. Her hand burned at the woman's touch. She yanked it away and clutched it to her chest. A sentry stepped in and seized the woman by the shoulders.

"Be gentle with her," Rosalie called out.

"You killed my master," the woman hissed through her teeth. "Damanius won't be gentle with you."

Rosalie's eyes grew wide with fear. Damanius was the god of dark magic. Not many believed in him. Most preferred to only believe in the "noble" gods – the ones who could help meet people's needs. But she believed in Damanius. She'd felt his presence the moment she'd met Lord Zebadiah. Her encounter with the woman left her dizzy and chilled.

"Are you okay?" one of the sentries asked.

"Yes, of course." She smiled, trying to shake off the feeling. "She just surprised me, that's all."

"We're still finding pockets of resistance," the sentry explained. He placed a firm hand on her shoulder. "But most people don't feel like she does."

"I know." She forced a smile. She removed her gardening gloves and put them in her apron pocket. "I'm suddenly feeling a bit worn out. I think I'll go lie down for a bit."

Rosalie's dreams were dark and vivid. In one she was standing in front of a cliff. Lord Zebadiah stood before her. Only he wasn't standing on land. He was floating far above the sea. His long, black robes billowed around him and his eyes burned blood red. "You can't escape me," he hissed.

When she woke up screaming, Ash cradled her in his arms, but she didn't find comfort there. Nothing felt as it should. Something was wrong. She just didn't quite know what it was.

As she laid in bed, fighting for sleep, she felt physically drained. She also felt numb – like the happiness had been sucked out of her. She stared over at Ash sleeping beside her. Not even seeing him brightened her mood. She curled up in a ball and clutched the emerald stone around her neck. She muttered a small prayer to as many of the gods as she could recall. By the time she fell back asleep, the pillow was damp with her tears.

"You don't look well," Ash told her in the morning. She was standing in front of the bathroom mirror, brushing out her hair. Staring at her reflection, he could see her eyes had a hollowed look and her cheeks were colorless.

She turned toward him and offered a wan smile. "Well, thank you."

He didn't smile back. Instead he cocked his head to the side and studied her. "You were having quite the nightmare last night. Want to talk about?"

She shook her head *no*.

"Don't shut me out, Roe."

"I'm not shutting you out," she snapped. "I'm just …" She set the hairbrush down. Her tone softened. "I'm just dealing." She closed the gap between them and gazed up at him. "I'm sorry. I'm not quite myself, but I'll get there."

He nodded. Although he hated to see her this way, he would take her any way he could get her. He cradled her face in his hands and bent down to kiss her lips. "I've almost lost you twice," he said, referring to the night she spent in the woods, and the day she was shot. "I'm not going to let either of us go through that again."

"You won't lose me Ash," she assured him. But inside she wondered if she was losing herself.

In the days that passed, Rosalie's mood did not improve. Despite her promise not to, she continued to drift further away. Physically, only a small scar remained as evidence of her near encounter with death. But her demeanor was markedly changed.

"I think I might be losing her," Ash confessed to Stryker. It had been weighing on him, how distant she'd been.

"You're just hitting a rough patch. My wife and I have been through a few."

"No, this is different. She isn't the same around me. It's like she doesn't trust me, or she's hiding something."

"What could it be?"

"I'm not sure. But I can tell, something's not right. And she's having these nightmares where she wakes up screaming."

"What are they about?"

"That's just it. She won't tell me."

Stryker scratched his chin, deep in thought. "Maybe she's having dreams about the battle and is too embarrassed to tell you. Rosalie's a strong person. I'm sure it's hard for her to admit when she's afraid of something."

Ash nodded but looked doubtful. "I want so bad to help her, but she won't let me. I thought she knew she could come to me about anything."

"Give her time, Ash. She'll come around. In the meantime, all you can do is be there for her."

"Speaking of your wife," Ash said, changing the subject.

Stryker chuckled. "I didn't realize we were."

A ghost of a smile appeared on Ash's lips. "Well, you mentioned the rough patch, and it got me thinking. When are you headed back home?"

"I'm not sure. I know how much I'm needed here."

"You should go."

Stryker shot him a sideways look.

Ash said, "Don't get me wrong, we need you, we do. But your wife and child haven't seen you in months. They'd want to know that you're okay. Go home. Take Dillinger with you." Then he grinned and slapped his friend on the back. "Go exaggerate what heroes you two were."

Stryker chuckled. "Well, I did pretty much single-handedly bring down this evil empire."

"That's the spirit."

Ash arranged a big sendoff for Stryker, Dillinger, and the others wishing to return home to their families. There was music, dancing, and all of Druin was invited to attend. Rosalie was all smiles when she joined

Ash at the event – even participated in a dance or two. But the moment Stryker and the others were gone, she became withdrawn and announced she was returning to her room to lie down. Ash hid his disappointment behind a strained smile and a flask of whiskey.

Over the next several days, Rosalie spent most of her time outdoors, hoping the fresh air would snap her out of her funk. She continued to help in the fields but soon realized the joy of planting had faded. She wondered if the memory of what the elderly woman told her was affecting her more than she'd first realized.

She tried assisting Othelia in the stables, expecting it to be like old times. But despite the hours the pair spent grooming the horses, she continued to feel numb. Othelia tried to carry the conversation with idle chitchat and gossip, but soon grew tired of Rosalie's lack of response or enthusiasm.

Before long, she stopped going to the stables. She stopped going outside altogether. She remained confined to her room and often didn't bother to get out of bed.

Dekler was called upon for his borrowing powers, but when he placed his hands on Rosalie, nothing happened. It was as if his powers were blocked by an impenetrable wall.

"Thank you for trying," Rosalie told him kindly. "And I never got a chance to thank you for saving my life."

"It was nothing," Dekler said, embarrassed.

"Nonsense. I know firsthand how much pain and energy it takes to heal someone." She paused, blanketed by an abrupt and unexplainable sadness. There was so much more she wanted to say but could no longer find the energy. Her mouth turned downward in a frown and her eyes closed.

Dekler squeezed her hand and concentrated hard. He felt no tingling sensation; no feeling at all. "I'm sorry I couldn't do more," he whispered in her ear before slipping out of the room.

As days stretched into weeks, Ash continued to try and give her space but his patience was reaching a tipping point.

CHAPTER THIRTY-SEVEN

A month had passed since the Liberation Alliance freed the Druins. Although many of the liberated *variants* returned to their villages, several stayed behind out of newfound loyalty to Ash. Ash and his men worked tirelessly to restore order. Most of the people continued to be won over by the kindness and steadfastness his men portrayed. People were anxious for a leader they could trust; one who had their best interest at heart.

Pockets of resistance continued to surface and were dealt with swiftly, but quietly. The newly planted crops were starting to take root. Ash's army worked hand-in-hand with the townspeople as a show of good will. The sound of laughter and children playing echoed through the castle halls – something that had been missing under Lord Zebadiah's reign.

Rosalie still hadn't recovered. Each night she screamed out in her sleep. When she awoke, she was covered in sweat. She'd never revealed to Ash what the nightmares were about, and he'd long since stopped asking about them. He told himself she'd reveal them when the time was right.

Talon had come to see Rosalie, at Ash's request. His hope was, upon seeing her old friend, Rosalie would cheer up, but Talon's presence did little to brighten her mood or improve her condition. He stuck around for a few days but couldn't stomach the drastic change in Rosalie and soon made excuses to return to Mabel Village.

Ash feared Rosalie would see Talon's quick departure as another betrayal, but she remained indifferent. She may not have noticed, but Ash vowed to never forget. Talon may have saved Rosalie in their youth, but in Ash's mind, the man lacked character in adulthood. He regretted his decision to invite him back, and hoped he'd never return.

"You're looking lovely this morning," Ash told Rosalie when she joined him for breakfast on the veranda. She wore a terrycloth robe. It was her standard wardrobe these days.

She forced a smile. "I feel much better." Her pale skin and dark circles under her eyes suggested her good health was exaggerated, but he didn't call her out on it.

"I sent some men out to find Lexis," he said, hoping it would spark some sort of emotion – curiosity, anger, he didn't care which at this point. "They found her at a nearby village. I've invited her to come back."

She sat up straighter in her chair. "And?"

"We'll see. She's still ashamed of the way she betrayed us. I let her know there were no hard feelings."

"Speak for yourself," Rosalie retorted, crossing her arms in front of her chest.

Ash grinned, happy to see some fire back in her. "Well, I figured if she came back you can give her a piece of your mind."

She nodded, then pressed her fingertips to her forehead. "I don't know why I don't feel right," she admitted. A tear rolled down her cheek. "When I first woke up after being shot…"

Wincing at the memory, Ash reached his hand across the table and gave hers a squeeze.

"…I felt pretty good. I mean, obviously I wasn't ready to jump up and do cartwheels, but I felt better than I've been feeling lately."

"The doctor said he can't find anything wrong." After Rosalie started to confine herself to her room, Ash had seen to it that a doctor checked in on her at least daily.

"But I know something's wrong," she said, frustrated and admitting it aloud for the first time, even to herself.

He squeezed her hand again. "Should I bring the doctor back in?"

"No," she shook her head and pulled her hand away. "I'm sick of doctors. I want to see Marx."

Ash squared his shoulders. He hadn't forgiven his old friend for letting Rosalie go into battle. But seeing her in this condition, he knew he'd need to mask any anger he held towards Marx – for her sake. He cleared his throat. "I'll send for him."

"You're going to do more than that," she said. "You're going to forgive him."

Marx came straight away. It came as a shock to him to see Rosalie in such poor shape. He'd heard rumors she hadn't been feeling well, but he was unprepared for the hollowness in her eyes and the lack of coloring in her cheeks and lips. She was perched in a chair, a blanket covering her legs. He bent down and hugged her, gently, as if she was a fragile doll, then stood and directed his attention towards Ash. The tension between the two men was almost palpable, and Rosalie rolled her tired eyes in frustration.

She rose slowly from her chair. When Ash tried to help her to her feet, she waived him off. "I am capable of standing by myself," she said. She looked rail thin and Ash wasn't so sure. Her body swayed and she rested a hand on the table to steady herself. "Now, if you don't mind, I'm going to take a shower while you two talk. When I get out, I want a private word with Marx." She shot both men a warning look — a look that said they'd better sort their issues out or they would have to deal with her.

Marx watched her walk away. "Still has spitfire," he offered.

"Yeah, but she's not the same."

"Many people who've been in battle never are."

"This is different." Ash raked his hands through his hair. "She's not as strong physically. She's pale, she's lost weight. It's as if something is slowly draining her."

"Has the doctor been in to see her?"

"Only about twice a day."

Marx sighed heavily and a grave silence fell over the two men. Surprising them both, Ash was the first to speak.

"Marx, you're one of my oldest friends. I may not like what you did, but I respect it. I also respect that Rosalie had a choice."

They stared at each other, neither knowing what came next.

"I guess what I'm trying to say," Ash continued, "is that I forgive you. I want things to be right between us."

Eyes flooding with tears, Marx stepped towards his friend. Without warning, he pulled him into a fierce hug. "Thank you," he said, the weight of Orthron lifting from his shoulders. "You don't know what that means to me."

When Rosalie returned from her shower, the two men were seated on the veranda, swapping stories and laughing. There was a peace between them.

"This is what I hoped to see," she said. "Now, if you don't mind," she told Ash, "I'd like a few words with Marx."

Marx raised an eyebrow. Ash opened his mouth to argue, thought better of it, then nodded in agreement. "I'll just go check on a few things," he said. He kissed her forehead, then made his exit.

"I'm happy to see you two getting along again," Rosalie told Marx once they were alone.

"Me too. It's been weighing heavily on me."

"I know, that's why I knew you needed to talk. I need your focus, and I knew I couldn't have it if you were all twisted up about where you stood with Ash."

"What do you need from me?"

Tears brimmed in her eyes. "I need you to see what's wrong with me." Her slender shoulders began to shake. She no longer had the strength to pretend she was okay.

"Hey, hey, don't cry. You're going to be fine."

"Do you know that … or do you hope that?" She sniffed and looked up at him, pleading for a solid answer.

Marx took her hand in his, trying to hide his shock at its frailty. He closed his eyes, straining to focus. It had been a while since he'd used his gifts. Ever since the battle, he'd been too twisted up inside to concentrate. As he held her hand, a chilling sensation ran through his palm and up his fingertips. With his eyelids closed, he saw waves of colors, deep reds and blacks, but nothing more.

"I don't see anything," he admitted.

She dipped her head. "That almost worries me more."

"What do you say you and I go for a walk? Clear our heads."

He stood from his chair, offered her his hand, and helped her up. He hooked his arm through hers, supporting her, and the pair walked down the steps of the veranda and towards the orchard. As they walked, Marx kept the conversation light. He needed Rosalie's mind off her troubles.

"I hear Ash is experimenting with a new berry crop this year," he said. "People are pretty excited about it. It's in high demand and expected to turn a large profit."

"Yeah, I've heard him mention that a time or two."

The further they walked away from the castle, the more Rosalie started to perk up. She began to joke around. Marx was laughing. The dark mood he'd carried over the past month had lifted. He turned to

Rosalie and patted her cheek. When he did so, he felt a wave of energy. And finally, finally, he could see clearly.

"Sorcery," he said excitedly once he, Ash, and Rosalie were back behind closed doors.

"Pardon?" Rosalie asked. She took a seat, drained from her walk and worried her legs would no longer support her.

"Lord Zebadiah had been using sorcery. He must have used it on Rosalie before he died."

"But that doesn't make any sense," she said, her excitement dissipating. "I was fine for a while. I only started feeling poorly a few weeks ago."

Ash and Marx were silent, contemplating.

"Did anything strange happen before you fell ill. Anything at all, even the slightest thing?" Marx asked.

She started to shake her head, no, but then a memory from her time working in the fields popped into her head. "There was this elderly lady," she said, shuddering at the horrible words the woman had spoken.

"Roe, she was just crazy," Ash said.

"No. I think it was more than that." She turned towards him and took his hand. "I didn't tell you because I didn't want to worry you; and I also know you don't believe in that sort of thing, but what she said to me … I think she was trying to put a curse on me."

"What did she say?" Marx asked. "Try to recall exactly."

"I'll never forget it. She said, 'Damanius won't be gentle with you.'"

Marx frowned. "Did she touch you?"

"Yes, she was squeezing my hand while she said it."

"That has to be it. She put a dark spell on you. Her curse may also be what's now blocking my visions from seeing your future."

"What makes you so sure?" Ash asked, feeling a sliver of hope despite not being a believer.

"Most dark spells are centralized to one location. This one seems localized to Castle Druin. Once Rosalie and I got away from here, she started to feel better and my visions returned. This place is stained with evil."

"Then we leave," Ash said, matter-of-fact.

Rosalie shook her head. "Ash, we can't. The people need us. We can't abandon them after we promised to help them."

"Rosalie's right," Marx said. "We don't leave."

"Then what?"

"We find a counter spell to reverse the curse, use it on Rosalie. Then. Then we cleanse this place."

Ash was readily on board with taking any measure to lift the curse that plagued the woman he loved. But convincing him of the merits of a cleanse for the entire castle proved harder than Marx anticipated. Rosalie, on the other hand, was willing to try anything. Ash eventually agreed to go along with the plan, mostly for Rosalie's sake, but it wasn't without a great deal of sarcastic comments and eye rolling.

Marx brought in a few trusted men to assist. Kipser, who had been with Rosalie when she was shot, was among them. Kipser didn't have a lot of experience with dark magic, and what he did know warned him to stay clear. But Rosalie was counting on him, and that was enough for him to swallow his reservations and do whatever was necessary to keep her safe. And healthy.

While Rosalie rested, Ash, Marx and his volunteers scouted out the castle library until they came across several dusty boxes in the back room. The boxes were jam-packed with old scrolls and spell books.

The men set the boxes out on the center library table. They emptied each box and worked feverishly to read through its contents.

"We start with finding a reversal spell for Rosalie," Marx said. "First one who finds it gets a beer on me."

Each man took a pile of scrolls and books and spread out. It would have been comical to see so many grown men astutely reading had the situation not been so dire. Hours passed without much progress. Then, as hope was fading, Kipser jumped up from the table, yelling excitedly. "I've got it."

Marx motioned him over to his table, clearing a spot for the large, leather bound book Kipser held open in his arms. Kipser placed it on the table, pointing to the open page. "Right here. That's it, right?"

Marx bent over to read the passage. The ink was faded, but he could still make out the words and rough sketches. His fingers skimmed over the crinkled page. "This is it," he said grinning. "Kipser, you come with me to see Rosalie. The rest of you," he said, looking around, "keep reading. Next we need to find the spell for cleansing the castle."

"We need her in the bath," Marx explained to Ash, showing him the page for the spell that he had ripped from the book.

"Over my dead body."

"Relax, she doesn't have to be naked. Although it might help…" he said, trying to cut the tension with indelicate humor.

Ash glared in his direction and Kipser cleared his throat, uncomfortable.

"We actually need her dressed in a white gown," Marx said more seriously. "We'll step out for a few moments so you can wake her up and she can get prepared."

Ash started a warm bath then gently nudged Rosalie awake. She looked so peaceful lying there. But with her ashen skin tone and diminishing frame, she was a pale reflection of her old self. He tucked a strand of her auburn hair behind her ear, the way he'd done a thousand times before. "I love you," he whispered before she awoke.

After getting out of bed and washing her face to wipe the sleep from her eyes, Rosalie dressed in the white gown she'd worn the day she'd regained consciousness. Ash helped her into the tub. "I feel sort of weird getting in fully clothed," she admitted.

He wanted to tease her that he'd feel sort of weird if she *wasn't* fully clothed, given she was about to be surrounded by other men, but he kept the sentiment to himself. It didn't seem the appropriate time for humor. Once she was in the bath, he opened the bedroom door and let Marx and Kipser back in. Marx headed straight for the vanity, opening the drawers and medicine cabinet, pulling out items, and inspecting them.

"Well there goes my privacy," Rosalie joked weakly.

"Sorry," Marx told her. "I'm looking for something with lavender in it." Once he found what he needed, he approached Rosalie and knelt beside her. He placed the back of his hand to her cheek. "We're going to make you better, okay?"

He sent Kipser to the kitchen to find olive oil while he sprinkled the lavender-infused shampoo into the water. When Kipser returned from the kitchen, Marx took the oil from him. He dumped most of it into the bath, but smeared part of it over Rosalie's forehead and atop her head. Then he retrieved the spell page from his left pants pocket and began to recite the words.

Cleansing water, cleansing oil
Purify the darkened soul
We stand united with courage bold
Release, release, the poisonous hold
Tainted blood and impure thralls
Fade away with our desperate calls
Powers vanquished; evil clutches rendered
Return this vessel to its former splendor

The spell was a half-chant, half-song. It required two people to perform in harmony, a role that Kipser was happy to fill. He'd always been a believer and had taken quite a liking to Rosalie. He'd been shocked to see how withdrawn and gaunt she was compared to the day she'd freed him from his cell in the lab.

Once the two men finished reciting the spell, Marx read from the page he was using as an instruction manual. "That first part was an external purification. This next part requires you to drink a liquid to purify you from the inside." He shot her an apologetic look.

- 253 -

"Bring it on," Rosalie said.

Alone with her thoughts and soaked gown, Rosalie changed into warm, dry clothes and began to brush out her hair. The oil hadn't been fully rinsed out and she sighed at the realization she'd be living with greasy hair for a week. Better than living under an evil curse, she supposed.

Marx returned soon after with a goblet full of an orange elixir that looked as thick as blood and smelled like rotting fish. He handed her the goblet, his unspoken apologies written on his face.

"What's in it?" she asked, taking a whiff, then holding the cup at a distance.

"It's best that you don't know."

"A new wine from our grape harvest?" she teased.

"Yeah, we'll go with that."

Rosalie closed her eyes and pressed the goblet to her lips. The smell was putrid – but the taste was worse. When the bitter liquid touched her tongue, she made a face and withdrew the glass. "I don't know if I can do this," she admitted.

"Roe, you have to," Ash spoke up.

"We can share it," she offered, shooting him a wink. She moved the glass to her lips once more. This time she didn't sip. She tossed the goblet back and began to chug. Her eyes were closed as she gulped down the shockingly revolting substance and did her best not to spit it back into the cup. *Mind over matter. Mind over matter.*

"I don't feel any different," Rosalie admitted once the ritual was over. Disappointment clouded her pretty face as her eyes brimmed with tears.

"We still need to cleanse this place," Marx assured her. He cupped her chin in his hand, forcing her to look at him. "Don't lose hope. This is going to work."

When Marx and Kipser returned to the library, they were pleased that the volunteers found a scroll that seemed to contain the cleanse they'd been searching for.

"Okay," Marx said to one of the men as he unrolled the scroll and studied it. "It says here that you have to sprinkle the perimeter with a mixture of salt and Trantilla oil. What the heck is Trantilla oil?"

"It's a plant oil," Kipser said. "Smells awful, but you can usually find it in a pharmacy. I wonder if there's any in the lab."

"I'll go check," Samtuana, one of the men offered.

He returned moments later with a bag of salt, a large bottle labeled *Trantilla*, an even larger, empty bottle, and a scientist from the lab. "He's here to help," he explained.

Normally Marx would object to inviting a stranger into his plans, but these were desperate times. "It's one-part salt, two-parts Trantilla oil," he said instead.

The scientist mixed the concoction in the empty bottle and stirred it before handing it to Marx. The bottle was heavy, but Marx wondered if it would be enough for the full perimeter of the castle.

"Great, let's go see what this stuff can do."

"What do I say if anyone questions what you are doing out there?" Ash said. Clearly, he still thought the ordeal was madness.

"Tell them it's weed killer. What do I care what you tell them?" Marx said crossly.

Marx used every last drop to surround the perimeter. Rosalie shuffled behind him, desperate to be part of the entire process. Once the Trantilla oil and salt converged with the soil, it gave off an awful smell.

"Smells like rotten eggs," Rosalie said, holding her nose. Although she felt physically tired, she was energized by the idea of ending whatever dark magic was causing her poor health.

"That means it's working," Marx told her.

"Really?"

He chuckled. "Actually, I have no idea."

Rosalie laughed, slapping him playfully on the arm. "What's next?"

"Next we have to dance naked around the castle."

"We what?" She looked surprised, but strangely, not horrified.

"I'm teasing. There's a chant I have to say over this place, and then, we wait."

"I'll help you with the chant," she offered solemnly.

"You should get some rest."

"I'll rest when the curse is lifted."

Marx, his two recruits, Rosalie, and the scientist all gathered to say the ancient chant believed to break the evil spell. Marx unraveled the scroll and was about to begin when Ash joined the group.

"I thought you weren't coming," Rosalie said.

"For you, I'd do anything." He smiled and squeezed her hand. He felt guilty that he'd given her and Marx such a hard time about it. The woman he loved needed his strength and support, not his snide remarks and skepticism.

"I know you've never believed in gods or evil curses. I appreciate that you try."

Marx cleared his throat, interrupting. "If you two lovebirds are ready, we can begin."

The chant was brief, but peculiar. Marx read it aloud slowly to the group, then they chanted aloud with him, repeating it three times as the scroll prescribed. Marx was tense as he enunciated every word. *Cleansing breath, cleansing spirits.*

Ash was a good sport, but in his head, he imagined whomever wrote the scroll was having the last laugh at their expense. *Salted wounds and healing oil.* It was all nonsense, in his mind.

When the chanting was over, the group dispersed. According to Marx, it would take until the next sunrise for any of their efforts to have an impact.

CHAPTER THIRTY-EIGHT

Rosalie awoke with the sun, feeling refreshed. The window in her room had been left open and she sat up in bed, breathing in the cool air. Beside her, Ash slept soundly. She bent down and kissed his cheek, then arose from bed and walked to the window. She looked out over the castle grounds, admiring the beauty of the fields for the first time. And then she felt it – the evil that had weighed her down was lifted. It was as if the darkness had been chased away by the dawn. She felt light. Rejuvenated.

Assuming Ash wouldn't believe her, she tiptoed to the bedroom door and slipped into the hallway. She knew Marx would be interested in the results of his efforts.

When she reached his room, he opened the door before she had time to knock. His silver hair was pulled back into a ponytail and he was sporting a huge grin. "I knew you were coming," he said.

"Was I that loud?"

"No, I mean I could *see* that you were coming." He lifted Rosalie off her feet and swung her around. He hugged her tight, then set her back down. "Sorry, I guess I was more excited than I thought."

She laughed. "I'm feeling much better too. It worked. I have to admit, I was a little skeptical."

"But you've always been such a firm believer."

She looked down, ashamed. "I guess my faith has been a bit tested these days."

"What did Ash say?"

She bit her lip and shot him a guilty look. "I haven't told him yet."

"What? Why?"

Her cheeks glowed pink. "Well, you saw him yesterday. He didn't believe in anything we were doing. I guess I needed to tell somebody who would believe me and not make me doubt."

"Well, you came to the right door," he laughed. "But Rosalie, you should tell him."

"Tell me what?" Ash spoke up from behind them, startling them both.

"You really have a gift for sneaking up on people," Rosalie told him crossly.

He stared at her. Then, for the first time in days, he offered a warm, genuine smile that reached his eyes and softened his features. "Roe, you look…"

The coloring had returned to her cheeks and lips and her face shone brightly. The dark circles under her eyes had disappeared. She had a healthy, radiant glow about her. Until this moment, he'd forgotten how dazzling she used to look; before the battle.

"Look what?" Her green eyes danced with humor for the first time in weeks.

"Beautiful," he said softly. He pulled her towards him and pressed his lips to hers. "It worked," he said in disbelief.

"It worked," she agreed.

"It's good to have you back."

"It's good to be back."

"If you two are done here," Marx interrupted, "I've got my own things to attend to." His tone was stern, but his eyes twinkled with amusement.

"I'm sorry to see that lifting this evil curse didn't cure your snarky attitude," Ash teased.

"No, but it did cure something else. My visions are back," he said, crossing his arms in front of his chest with pride.

"That's good news. Now what do you see for us?" Ash asked, slinging an arm around Rosalie's slim shoulders and pulling her in close.

"Hmm… red-headed children?" He grinned, and Ash snorted.

"For you two," Marx said, growing more thoughtful. "I only see great things."

"Give it to me straight," Ash teased, "is she going to be more trouble than she's worth?"

Laughing, Marx shot back, "I don't think you need my visions to know the answer to that."

"Hey now," Rosalie spoke up. "He isn't exactly easy to get along with either."

"That I also don't need a vision to confirm."

Once Ash and Rosalie were alone in their room, Ash's mood turned pensive. He pulled her into in his arms and gazed down at her. "Marx was right you know?"

"About what?" Her cheeks flushed with the exhilaration of his embrace.

"I don't need his visions to know we're going to be great together."

Her lips curved into a smile as she stared up at him. "Neither do I."

He swept her hair back from her face, then bent down and kissed her lips. She shuddered with pleasure as his thumbs caressed her jawline.

"I love you Roe," he told her, his heart breaking at how close he'd come to losing her. "Always and forever."

"I love you too, Ash," she whispered back. Her mind wandered back to the day she'd first met him – the puzzling combination of foreboding and attraction she'd felt. Things were so different now from then, but the same thrilling anticipation stirred within her. "I'm glad you found me that day," she said wistfully, her eyes misting.

Blue eyes burning with desire, Ash said, "No, Roe. That day we found each other."

He stroked her cheek, and when his lips met hers once more, he closed his eyes and felt the familiar rush of admiration and desire. He'd fallen harder than he'd meant to, harder than he'd thought possible. But he had no complaints about where he'd landed – in the arms of a woman he would forever love and cherish.

Acknowledgements

The idea for ASH FALLEN came to me while I was vacationing on the Oregon Coast; so first and foremost I'd like to thank my friends and family who joined me on that trip and were not offended whenever I snuck away to get my ideas out on paper.

An enormous thank you to my sister, Melissa, who promotes my books with fervor, forces me to get out of my comfort zone to attend book signings, and has dubbed herself my "number one fan." Thank you to my two brothers, Justin and Ryan, who used their artistic abilities to give the book a final polish (even though romance is *not* their genre … but it should be, am I right?). And to my parents, Craig and Debbie, for providing their home as a haven for me to write and bounce ideas off them.

To the readers – thank you. Thank you for coming along with me on this journey. Thank you to those who read early versions of the novel and offered encouragement and feedback along the way. To the loyal readers who ask, "When's your next book coming out so I can have something to read?" – you'll never know how much that question means to me.

As always, a special thank you to my husband, Joe, and two beautiful daughters, Kiersten and Bella. You sacrifice the most and deserve the most praise. Thank you for being my support system as I pursue my dreams of being an author.

About the Author

Blake Channels was born in Tri-Cities, Washington where she resides today with her husband and two children. She graduated from Washington State University and is a wife, mother, and finance professional by day and a writer in her heart and soul – and whenever her schedule allows. In addition to writing romance novels, Blake enjoys spending time with family and friends, soaking up the sun, camping, and curling up with a good book.

Books by Blake Channels

❖ Darkened (Romantic Suspense)

❖ The Comforts (Sci-Fi Romance)

❖ Ash Fallen (Fantasy Romance)

Visit blakechannels.com to learn more about the author and available books.

Made in the USA
Columbia, SC
10 May 2023

16369612R00167